The Promise of Paradise

BY

Allie Boniface

This is a work of fiction. Names, characters, places, and incidents are either the product of the author's imagination or are used fictitiously, and any resemblance to actual persons living or dead, business establishments, events, or locales, is entirely coincidental.

The Promise of Paradise

COPYRIGHT © 2013 by Allie Boniface

All rights reserved. No part of this book may be used or reproduced in any manner whatsoever without written permission of the author. Note: this book was previously released as *Lost in Paradise* with The Wild Rose Press (publication date 2007). Changes in scene and character accompany this re-released version.

Cover Art by Renee Rocco

Visit the author at www.allieboniface.com
Contact the author at allieb@allieboniface.com

Published in the United States of America

Dedication

For all my writing friends, who've supported me through thick and thin in this unpredictable business of storytelling. Follow your dreams, believe that you can, and never stop re-inventing yourselves!

Chapter One

"Is this it?" Jen craned her neck and stared at the street sign.

Ashton wiped one damp palm on her thigh and tried to will away the knots in her stomach. "I don't know." She pulled her Volkswagen to the curb and dug in her pocket for the email printout with directions. "Next right after the town green." She looked across the street. Don's Convenience Store waved a limp awning in the afternoon heat. "Across from Don's. Yeah, this is it. It's gotta be."

Already out of the car, Jen walked to the corner. Pulling her platinum blonde hair into a ponytail, she checked the crooked street sign and nodded at her best friend.

Ash made the turn and parked. "First house on the right," she read aloud. "Number two."

She leaned her forehead against the steering wheel and closed her eyes. Deciding not to take the job at Deacon and Mathers was one thing. Moving to an unknown town a hundred miles from her parents, fleeing the scandal that now appeared in every Boston newspaper, was something else altogether. The knots in her stomach multiplied and stretched fingers of steel that began to strangle her heart.

"Ash?" Jen poked her through the open window. "You okay?"

She raised her head and forced herself to take a deep breath. "I don't know."

Jen pulled open the car door. "Come on. Let's look at the place."

Shoving dark blonde curls from her forehead, Ash got out of the car and stopped. "What if I've made a mistake? Like the biggest possible mistake in the world?" She stared up at the house, a nondescript two-story with dusty windows. It didn't look like anything she'd ever seen before. *Well, that's the point, right? I wanted something completely different. I wanted to start fresh, someplace where no one knew me.*

Willing her feet to step one in front of the other, she followed Jen to the front porch. "What if I'm really supposed to open my own law practice, go into politics, like Jess and Anne? Like Dad?" She sank onto the bottom porch step.

Jen tried the door. "You're not," she said over her shoulder.

"How do you know?"

"Because you spent the last two months of law school miserable and because you need a change."

"My parents are going to kill me."

Jen joined her on the step. "To tell you the truth, I think your parents have other things on their minds these days."

Like explaining to the press why my father was caught with drugs and a nineteen-year-old prostitute in his car? Two months before he was about to receive the Democratic vice-presidential nomination? Ash dug her toe into the pavement, tracing cracks and watching ants scurry. "I guess you're right." Suddenly, her decision to leave Boston and the center of the Kirk family scandal didn't seem like the worst decision in the world. In fact, when she thought about it, it seemed downright practical.

She eyed the car and wondered how long it would take her to unpack. Not that long. The apartment was supposed to be furnished, and she'd brought only a few clothes and books. Most of the memories she'd put into storage or burned.

Jen worked her fingernail beneath some peeling paint on the porch railing. "You need this, Ash, a summer to yourself. You need to be..." She stopped for a moment, as if searching for the right word. "...away."

"Away from the media circus? Or away from Colin?"

Jen didn't answer, and for just a moment, Ash let herself ache with the memory of Colin Parker, her love all through law school. She'd planned to accompany him to Europe and then move in with him at the end of the summer. Hell, she'd planned on marrying him. But Colin had dumped Ash thirty-seven days earlier with a note tucked into her planner.

I need some time and space to think... it began and ended with his scrawled signature minus *Love* or any other word that suggested he'd shared her bed and her heart for the last three years.

One month before graduation, and three weeks after the debacle with her father, he'd dumped her. A tear snuck its way down her cheek, and Ash dropped her head to hide it. The breakup hadn't been the worst of it. Colin hadn't needed time. He'd lied about that part. He *had* needed space, though, space in which to date Callie Halliway, president of the Student Activities Council and Colin's co-author on a half-dozen journal articles. Beautiful and well-pedigreed, Callie partnered him perfectly, both on his arm and his resume. Ash had been replaced just like that, one day there and the next day gone, as if she'd never even existed in Colin's life.

Jen elbowed her. "Take a look at this."

With effort, Ash raised her head. Emerging from the cornflower blue house across the street was a short, stocky woman. White hair sprang out from her head in every direction, and she wore bright yellow gardening gloves. Without slowing, she marched down her walk and across the street. Up their crooked pavement she came, until she stopped in front of them. Though barely five feet tall, she towered over Ash and Jen sitting on the step, and Ash felt suddenly as if she were back in second grade, with an angry Miss Howard staring at her across a cluttered room. A frown carved the woman's wrinkled face into disapproving lines, and beady brown eyes examined them. Ash wasn't sure whether to laugh or run and hide.

The woman propped both hands on her hips and said nothing. Jen stood, and Ash followed. "Hi there. I'm Asht-Ashley Kirtland." She corrected herself, changing her name at the last minute. With the Kirk name splashed across every paper in the Northeast, she didn't need anyone connecting her to it.

The woman nodded. "Helen Parker." She pointed across the street. "Lived there for thirty-two years, this spring. I take care of this place and the one next door. You have any problems, come see me." She paused and massaged one temple with a gnarled hand. "Up the block there, in the white house near the end, live the MacGregors. Hiram drinks too much, but his wife Sadie's a doll, so no one says too much about it. He's harmless, anyway."

Ash slid a glance toward Jen. No secrets here. That didn't bode well.

"Two houses down from that is Lanie Johnson's. Used to be a Rockette, or some such thing, 'til she busted her hip and ended up back here in Paradise. Had a man at one point, a while back, but he ran off two or three years ago."

Helen paused to draw a breath. White flecks of spittle marked the edges of her mouth. "The rest of these homes are rentals, mostly to college kids during the year." She narrowed her eyes, and Ash read the woman's message loud and clear.

"I just graduated," she explained, leaving off the bit about Harvard and law school. "I'm subletting for the next three months."

Helen's mouth relaxed a fraction. "Well, the other places are empty now." Her gaze moved from the girls to the door behind them. "You're the only ones living here this summer, far as I know."

"Really?" Loneliness dropped a curtain over Ash's hopes of finding new friends. Well, solitude was probably better if she hoped to figure out what direction her life was supposed to take now.

Helen reached into her front pocket and pulled out a key ring. Dangling it from two fingers, as if it were a dirty tissue, she held it out. "Square one's for the front door. Smaller one's for your door upstairs. And the silver one opens your mailbox." She glanced at the solitary car by the curb. "Where's the other one?"

Ash looked up from the keys, confused at the question. "I'm sorry?"

Helen puffed out a long breath of air. "The other *tenant*." She rubbed her forehead with one hand, as if trying to pull the name from memory. "Edward something. Your downstairs housemate."

"I have a housemate?" Ash looked at Jen, who grinned.

Helen had already headed down the front walk, but at the question, she turned back. "Of course. I thought you'd be arriving together." She eyed the porch for a moment, and Ash read the look in her watery blue eyes: *You better behave.*

She stifled a laugh. "Thank you, Helen. Nice meeting you."

The woman turned without replying and shuffled across the street, where she vanished beyond the sunflowers cloaking her front door.

"Cool. A housemate," Jen said. "A *male* housemate."

"Just what I need," Ash said as she tried the key in the door. "Come on. We've got stuff to unpack."

Chapter Two

"I wonder what he looks like," Jen said as they pulled sheets and pillowcases from a cardboard box.

"He's probably seventy-five years old, newly widowed, and blind in one eye." Ash stood on the bed and stretched to hang a curtain over the back window.

Jen collapsed onto paisley-patterned pillows. "Why do you do that?"

"Do what?"

"Find the worst in everything. He could be young and single, you know. Why not?"

Ash sat too. "Because if he's really young and single, why would he be living here?"

Jen turned to Ash, lips still but eyes sending the message.

"Yeah, I know." Ash shrugged. "But I'm a special case. A nut case. I'm sure most people in this town aren't from screwed up families like I am."

"You never know." Jen bounced off the bed and changed the subject. "Hey, let's check out the porch roof. That's the best part about this place. I saw it online, in the pictures. Come on."

Ash followed Jen into the kitchen and leaned against the refrigerator. "It's probably unsafe."

Her friend tugged at the oversized window beside the sink. "It's not unsafe. If it was, they couldn't rent the house." The window pulled free, and in another minute she had climbed through onto the second-floor rooftop that stretched across the front of the house.

"Be careful." Ash edged closer and peeked outside.

"Oh, please. Stop being such a worrier. It's safe." Jen walked the perimeter of the roof and peered over to the street below. "This railing is brand new. Look." She turned at Ash's silence. "Get your ass out here right now and look at this view."

Ash propped her elbows on the sill and shook her head. "I'm afraid of heights."

"Not anymore you're not. Not with this roof." Jen slid to a seat and crossed her legs. "You could have one heck of a party out here."

Ash stayed where she was. She wasn't really afraid of heights. She was more afraid of not knowing what lay out there, of the too-wide sky that stung her eyes with its brightness and threatened to swallow her up. Right this moment, she didn't feel like taking new steps anywhere, not even ten feet outside her kitchen window.

Jen began to drum her heels against the roof. Sighing, Ash pulled herself up and over the window sill. One deep breath. Then another. *Okay*. Not so bad after all. With careful steps, she walked from one end of the roof to the other. Beyond the back lawn of her rental house, the center of Paradise, New Hampshire, rose to greet her, a picturesque town with an old-fashioned Main Street and two stone churches squatting on the town green. To her left, Lycian Street meandered below. In the distance she could make out the tops of red brick buildings over at the town's junior college. She took a deep breath and peeked over to the sidewalk.

"Wow." From here she could see all the way to the street's end in both directions. Maybe this hadn't been the wrong decision after all. Standing close enough to reach the leaves that swayed above her, Ash felt peaceful for the first time in months. She closed her eyes and drew it all in, the quiet street, the sleepy town. Somehow, it felt right. It felt like a good place to spend a summer. It felt like a good place to escape the mudslinging, a good place to figure out how to tell her parents she wanted a different life than the one they'd sketched out for her from birth.

Most of all, it seemed like a good place to forget her heartache, to try and flee the ghosts of Colin and Callie that reappeared every time she turned a corner.

Ash slid to a seat beside her friend. "Okay, maybe you're right. Might not be a bad place for a party." *If I'm ever in the partying mood again.*

"Told you." Jen glanced at her watch. "What else do you need me to do? I'm going down to visit the family this weekend. Gotta help my little brother mend a broken heart."

"Lucas? What happened? "

"Dumped his fiancée. He found her in bed with someone else." Jen's face went dark.

"Aw, poor guy. That stinks." She'd always had a soft spot for Jen's little brother – not that *little* was the right word, since the guy towered over both of them. "When?"

"Last month." Jen pulled her hair onto the top of her head before letting it fall again. "It's okay. He's better off without her."

Ash rested one cheek in her hand. Looked as though it had been a rough spring for break-ups. Maybe Lucas needed to find a Paradise of his own to escape to for a little while.

"Anyway, I think the last train back to the city leaves in an hour or so," Jen went on. "So you need anything? Want to make a run to the grocery store before I go?"

"Nah. I'll find one tomorrow."

"You sure? I can just hang out for a while if you want."

The thought tempted her. Despite her need to be alone and sort through the snarl of feelings around her heart, despite the funny, run-down house that was already starting to seem like home, part of her wanted Jen to stay. Ash opened her mouth to answer, but a roar from below drowned out her words.

"What the hell is that?" Jen turned to peer through the slats in the railing. A second later, she pulled herself to her feet and leaned over as far as she could. A grin spread itself across her face. "Whoa. Take a look at this."

"What?"

But Jen didn't answer and instead just stared.

Curious, Ash joined Jen at the railing and looked down. Near the curb, engine still running and rock music bellowing from the speakers, idled a red pickup truck. White and yellow flames danced along both sides. Bending over the tailgate was a broad, bare, definitely male back. *Yow.* No wonder Jen looked like she was about to start drooling. Even one floor up, Ash could trace the outline of nearly every muscle in his arms and back. A bright red and yellow king cobra tattoo curled around his left triceps. Wavy brown hair fell across the sides of his face. His jeans, faded in all the right places, sat low on his hips. Ash squinted harder and ran a hand over her hair.

Oh God. They still make men who look like that?

"Turn around, please," Jen commanded under her breath. As if he'd heard her, he straightened, biceps flexing as he hauled two large boxes from the back of the truck and turned into the sidewalk. Her sidewalk. He looked up, and Ash's heart dove into her stomach. A neatly trimmed goatee underscored a crooked nose. He flashed a smile and winked.

"Hey," he called. "You live here?"

Jen nodded and jabbed a thumb in Ash's direction. "She does."

"I'm Eddie West. Movin' in today." It was hard to hear him over the noise of the truck's humming engine and the music. Ash watched his mouth move instead.

"Need any help?" Jen asked.

Eddie shook his head. "Nah. I've just got a couple of boxes to bring in. The rest is coming tomorrow. But thanks." He continued up the sidewalk.

Jen cupped her hands around her mouth and yelled down. "Come up later if you want."

Ash elbowed her. "What are you doing?"

Eddie backpedaled and nodded, grinning wider. As he disappeared from their view, the heavy front door creaked open and, after a few seconds, thudded shut behind him.

Jen straightened. "See? I told you he'd be good-looking." She rolled her eyes. "He's beyond good-looking, Ash." She fell back against the railing, hands to heart in a dramatic pantomime. "He's perfect."

But she wasn't sure a good-looking housemate was what she needed this summer. Hadn't she sworn off men just a few weeks ago? "I'm sure he's not perfect, Jen. You don't even know if he's available. Maybe he has a girlfriend. Maybe he's *married*."

"He's not. He wasn't wearing a ring."

"How do you know?"

"I looked."

"From ten feet up you looked?"

Jen winked, grinning. A few minutes later, the pickup's music squawked off. Less than two minutes after that, footsteps thundered up the stairs, and a fist pounded on Ash's front door. *Already? He's coming up to visit already?* Her heart crept from a steady gallop to a sprint. She didn't need to meet anyone new, not now. She needed to get her head straightened out. She needed to heal. She needed to –

"Are you getting that?" Jen stood perfectly still and stared at her.

"Fine." She crawled back through the open window, crossed the living room, and stood before the door. *Please don't be perfect. Please have one lazy eye or a limp or something caught in your teeth or...*

Ash opened the door, and Eddie stood on the other side, smiling.

A breeze kicked through the living room, one of those warm summer gusts that sweep in from nowhere. It lifted the hair off her neck and blew a puff of dust across the doorstep. For an instant, the room seemed to widen, to swell with warmth, and sun flooded the space.

Wow. Maybe Jen is right. Maybe he is perfect.

Eddie wasn't tall, but the faded green t-shirt he'd put on outlined every muscle she could see. Sweat lined the creases in his forehead, and brilliant blue eyes met hers. Their color startled her, so bright they made the summer sky seem shady and dull. The more she examined them and tried in vain to match them to a Crayola color that had never existed, the more she felt a strange tumbling in her stomach.

God, what's wrong with me? He's just a guy. Pull it together, Ash. Taking a deep breath, she shifted her gaze to the doorjamb above him. "Hi, Eddie. Come on in."

He didn't move for a moment, just stood and studied her. Cocking his head, he wiped his forehead against the sleeve of his shirt, then stepped across the threshold and into Ash's life. Maybe it was the sun, maybe the odd wind that had picked up at just that moment, but suddenly she had the strangest urge to reach over and touch him, to run one finger along his brow and down his cheek. She studied a wrinkle in the fold of his shirt and wanted to smooth it. Something hovered in the space between them, and a strange sense of closeness pierced her throat and stopped her words.

"Are you – ?"

"When did – ?"

They spoke at the same time, but the words fell away, and though neither finished a thought, they both began to laugh.

Eddie reached for Ash's hand. "Nice to meet you."

She placed her palm in his, for a moment only, but she liked the way it felt. Warm. Safe. "I'm-uh-Ashley. Ash." Again she altered her first name, and didn't offer her last, in case he'd been watching the news lately. And who hadn't?

* * *

Ash studied her new housemate as Jen joined them in the living room. Eddie leaned in the doorway, cracking his knuckles, and continued to smile at her. He was saying something, about the weather or maybe the house, but she couldn't concentrate over the thumping of her heart. She watched him, though. She watched as Eddie's goatee moved when he spoke, a rich, wide spread of stubble that covered his chin. She wondered for a moment what it would be like to feel it against her own cheek, and a tickle ran up the back of her neck.

Ash pushed the thought away. *Forget it.* The pain of Colin still stung, and even a friendly neighbor with rugged, take-your-breath-away good looks couldn't chase that memory from her mind.

She tore her gaze away to turn and look behind her, seeing for the first time the furniture that filled her new living room. A loveseat sat under the wide window overlooking the street, with a worn corduroy couch opposite it. A tall bookcase stood in one corner near the kitchen, and two oak end tables completed the set. Hmm. She might have to invest in a few pieces of furniture after all. Ripped boxes and limp garbage bags covered the floor. She blushed, embarrassed.

"I just moved in. Sorry about the mess."

Eddie shrugged. "What mess?"

Her smile returned. "Want a seat?"

He nodded and made his way to the couch, stepping over a box and around a stack of books. Jen plopped down beside him. Hands laced behind her head, she stretched out her short legs and grinned at Eddie. Jen had always been good at that, sliding up to men without a second thought. Ash wished sometimes she could be more like her friend, instead of sitting in the shadows and thinking too much. She'd never had to work to get Colin, anyway. He'd showed up on her doorstep three days after she arrived at Harvard.

"So you're Senator Kirk's daughter," he'd said, and that was that. The following day they went out for coffee. The next weekend she took him home to meet her parents. They hadn't been apart since.

Ash's eyes burned, and she reached up to rub away the tears she knew would appear in another minute. She found a spot on the loveseat and forced her attention to Jen and Eddie, in an effort to steer her mind back to the conversation instead of the thoughts running around inside her head.

"Nice place, huh? I mean the house, the street, and all." Eddie waved to the ceiling above them as he leaned back, settling himself into the cushions.

Ash followed the movement and noticed strong, calloused hands, with scars on the knuckles, and one pinky finger bent in an odd way. Warmth filled her belly. She always noticed men's hands. Maybe that's why she found baseball players and cellists so sexy. She liked hands that looked powerful and rugged. Hands that could take on the world and throw it into its place when needed. Strong hands that turned soft when they wound their way along her body late at night. Eddie's hands looked like that.

The warmth reached her cheeks again, and she willed it away, afraid it would betray her.

"So how'd you end up moving in here?" Jen asked him.

"Mmm...long story."

She propped one elbow on the back of the couch. "We've got time."

Eddie's face changed a little, and he switched the subject, smooth as cream. "What about you, Jen?"

"What about me?"

"You and Ashley. What's your story? You guys from around here?"

Ash cringed a little when he said the name. *Ashley.* Her alias. The one she'd just made up to take the place of her true identity for the next few months. Already she felt guilty about lying to the guy who would be sharing her house. Damn. Why couldn't things ever work out the way she planned?

"Not really," she began, with a quick glance at Jen. How did she answer his question without revealing too much? "I mean, we just graduated and..."

"I grew up in Connecticut," Jen finished for her. "Ash is from outside Boston. I'm starting my residency next month, but the smart one here decided to take a summer to herself. You know, enjoy some peace and quiet. I just came along today for the ride." She leaned in closer. "That, and to interview any housemates she might have. To make sure they pass inspection."

Eddie looked at Ash. "And do I pass?"

Her cheeks got even hotter, and she wondered if that was answer enough.

Jen smiled. "Oh, I'd say you do."

He shook his head. "Good. I guess."

"Do you work in town?" Ash asked.

"Yep. Frank's Imports. It's a repair shop out by the highway. Some high-end stuff, Mercedes and Beamers, but mostly family cars. Hondas, Toyotas...lotta minivans." He grinned, and Ash nearly lost herself again.

"I think we passed it on the way in. Didn't we?" Jen asked.

A repair shop? Something tugged at the corners of Ash's mouth. Wouldn't her father die if he knew who his youngest daughter was living with? Not exactly the Stepford Club, she thought, and then was sorry, as if she'd somehow betrayed Eddie though she'd only just met him.

"I think I saw it," she said. "Big place. Red sign." Lawyer's eyes noticed everything, Ash's father used to tell her. Even the details. Especially the details.

Eddie nodded. "That's the place."

Her gaze returned to his face as he and Jen continued to talk, and Ash noticed with surprise that it was scarred in places. Besides a crooked nose, three thin scars ran almost parallel down the left side of his jaw. A thicker scar underlined his right eye, and peeking from beneath the left side of his goatee, a tiny spider web of lines faded into his upper lip.

God, what happened to him? Pain immeasurable echoed on that skin, and she was surprised she hadn't noticed the scars sooner. Ash shifted in the loveseat. Somehow, though, they didn't mar Eddie's appearance. Rather, they added character to eyes that danced and a voice that caressed like deep cello tones, mellow and laughing through the low notes on the scale.

After a few minutes, he stood. "I have a lot more to unpack," he said. "Sorry. Just wanted to say hi."

"Well, nice meeting you," Jen said. "You'll have to come back up later on."

His smile widened at the invitation, and a dimple winked below his deepest scar. "Sounds good." Eddie backed across the threshold. The door swung shut behind him, and the room seemed emptier than ever.

"Wow." Jen dropped onto the loveseat beside Ash and feigned lightheadedness. "If you don't find a way to sleep with that guy by the end of the summer, I give up."

"Good God, Jen. I'm not here to sleep with anyone." Ash tried to sound convincing. "This is my summer to heal, to get away from my parents. To forget about Colin. And figure out what I'm going to do with the rest of my life."

Jen opened one eye. "Speaking of which, when are you going to tell them?"

Ash studied her short, bare fingernails. "Which part? That I'm living in a no-name town instead of taking the job at Deacon and Mathers? Or that I'm thinking of changing my last name because my father can't keep his zipper closed? Or that precious Colin Parker isn't going to be their son-in-law after all?" She chewed at a hangnail. "I was kind of hoping to make it until July, at least."

"You talk to your parents every week."

"I know." The hangnail began to bleed.

Jen jumped up. "Let's get this room set up, anyway. Then I'll take off."

Ash waved a hand. "Don't worry about it. Go on home and let Lucas pour his heart out."

Jen laughed. "I am a good big sis, aren't I?"

"The best. You're sure you don't want a lift to the train station?"

"Nah. It's right down the block. I'll walk." Jen piled the empty boxes in one corner. "And Ash?"

"What?"

"I meant what I said. I know the last few weeks have been hard. You've got a gorgeous guy living downstairs from you. So have some fun this summer." She paused. "You can't hide away forever."

"It's only been five weeks. That's not forever."

"You know what I mean." She backed through the door before Ash could respond. "Bye. Call me later."

"Bye. And Jen?"

"Yeah?"

"If you run into my parents or one of my sisters in the city..."

"I know, tell them I don't know anything."

"At least for right now."

"No problem." Jen grinned and slipped away.

Ash closed her eyes and listened to her friend's footsteps disappear. Sleep with her downstairs neighbor? No way. Her head fell back onto the cushions, and she let them cradle her tired muscles. Despite her fatigue, thoughts of all kinds wound their way into her head. Colin. Callie. Her father. Eddie. *Yummy,* she thought before she could help herself. *And I don't usually fall for guys so fast.*

She rested one arm against her forehead. Who was she kidding? She never fell, period. She took careful steps. She analyzed all the possibilities. She played her cards one at a time, over long, slow days of contemplation. She never jumped into anything.

But maybe Jen was right this time. Ash had changed her name and slipped on a new skin. She'd moved to a new town where not a soul knew her. Why shouldn't she change a few other things? She pulled at her bottom lip with one finger. Maybe she should forget about the summer of chastity she'd promised herself. Maybe she should she lose herself in a different world for the next few months. She stared at the door, imagining Eddie a few steps away, unpacking boxes with muscles that flexed and strained and...

Oh God. What on earth would she tell him, if she did invite him up? She couldn't confess who she really was. Ashton Kirk? As in Senator Kirk's daughter? He'd look at her like she had two heads.

Rock music started up again, shaking the floor of her apartment a little before the volume lowered to a gentle throb. Smiling, she wondered about her new housemate. Something told Ash she wasn't the only one with a story. Why had Eddie moved into the house? Like her, was he only killing time for the summer? Or had he moved to tiny, protected Lycian Street to escape something or someone?

And what, for God's sake, had happened to him to leave such deep scars on an otherwise handsome face?

Chapter Three

Eddie finished pulling the sheets over his bed and flopped onto his back. He stared at the ceiling, where a few cracks spread above him and down the wall into the doorframe. Near the floor they widened and fractured the wood, causing the door to no longer shut tight. He studied the spaces just above the floor and imagined spiders shuttling in and out, making odd little homes inside the crevices of his apartment. Might be nice to disappear one day inside a wall, hang his head for a while until the blood-rush chased away faces from the past.

He turned to look through the wide window next to him. Far enough from his parents' house, but a ten-minute drive from work, he'd snapped up this place the minute he saw it advertised in the *Paradise Chronicle*. Didn't know he'd be sharing the house with another tenant, but hell, he didn't mind. Not when the other tenant looked like Ashley Kirtland did. Ebony eyes, honey-colored waves of hair falling around her face, a cute little waist that curved down to the longest pair of legs he'd ever seen…damn. He wouldn't mind looking at that body every morning over coffee, that was for sure. Ash seemed a little quieter than the women he usually dated, but she had a great smile and eyes you could drown in.

Eddie continued to stare out the window and wondered who else lived on the street. Only two blocks from the junior college on the hill, the homes rented mostly to college kids, he supposed. He guessed he'd have to cover his windows once fall rolled around, but right now he didn't have any curtains or blinds. He turned over and buried his face into the single pillow he'd brought with him.

Yeah, Ash seemed cool. It might be nice to have a housemate he could hang out with. Then again, he wasn't very good at just hanging out with women. Friendships with them always turned into relationships. He couldn't help it. He loved women. Loved watching them walk. Loved listening to them laugh. Loved feeling their hands clutching his back on a summer night, fingernails leaving red lines of passion down his spine.

Eddie got up and headed into the kitchen, where he flipped on the light and ran the faucet as high as it would go. He stuck his head under the running water and slurped. It tasted good and felt even better running down the sides of his face. He shook his head. Droplets flew and dappled the walls.

Wandering back into the living room, he looked around. High-ceilinged, with windows that faced the street, the place gave him a feeling of open space, something he hadn't had in a long time. He'd stayed at home too long, after the accident. At first he pretended his parents needed him around to get the bills in order, repair the back porch, take care of other things that had started to fall apart. But after almost three years, they didn't need him hanging around anymore. At twenty-seven, it was time for Eddie to start making a place of his own.

He ran his fingers through his damp hair, then turned and punched the wall. "Damn!" But he wasn't sure if he swore because of the pain radiating up his wrist or the grief of losing Cal that still caught him in the gut so hard he lost his breath.

Turning, he looked for a box to unpack. Anything to get his mind occupied with something else. He pushed aside one, pulled open another, and saw his brother's face staring up at him. Eddie stopped breathing. Taken four or five years ago, the two of them were forever frozen in that silver picture frame, tossing a football around the back yard and laughing at their mom. *She always snuck up on us and took our picture. We used to hate it.* He ran one finger over the glass. *Now I wish she'd taken a thousand more.*

Eddie tucked the picture into the box, facedown, and shoved the flap back into place. Surrounded by pictures of the past was the last place he wanted to be right now. He headed for the shower instead, doing his best to scrub away the memories.

Better, he thought as the hot water turned cool after awhile. At least he wasn't feeling so damned depressed anymore. He dropped his towel on the floor, dug through a suitcase for a change of clothes, and ran a comb through his damp hair. Then he darted upstairs and pounded a fist on his new housemate's door. Ash was absolutely the kind of distraction he needed right now.

* * *

"Hello?" Eddie knocked a second time and still heard nothing. Maybe Jen and Ash had gone out after all. He turned to leave.

"Eddie?" The door cracked open, and Ash peeked out. A hesitant smile lit her face. "Hi. Come on in."

"Thought maybe you guys were out."

"Jen left," she said. "She wanted to get back to the city before dark."

"You eat yet?"

She shook her head. "I was just wondering what Paradise has in the way of take-out."

"Well, there's Primo's Pizza down the block. Or Louie's Sub Shop around the corner. They're both close enough." The curiosity on Ash's face stopped him. "What?"

She smiled. "You live here." It wasn't a question, but a quiet discovery.

"Oh, yeah." Eddie nodded. "My whole life. Thought I mentioned it before. I grew up on the other side of town." He scratched the back of his neck. "Figured it was about time I moved out of my parents' house."

She looked at him a moment longer, but he couldn't read her thoughts. Judging? Wondering?

"Pizza," she decided after a moment. She looked over her shoulder, in the direction of the kitchen. "You know, there's a pretty cool rooftop out there. Want to get it to go, bring it back here?"

"Now you're talking." Eddie said, stomach growling.

"I don't have anything in the fridge," she apologized. "We should pick up a six-pack or something, too."

"Pizza and beer? A woman after my own heart."

Her cheeks reddened at his words, and Eddie grinned. He liked having that effect on women, making them at first uncomfortable around him and then by turns so comfortable he could open them up, peel back the layers, and turn their hearts inside out. He liked making women ache for him. He was good at it.

"You have a boyfriend?" he asked as he followed her down the stairs. He figured he might as well negotiate his options from the start.

She shook her head, and waves of hair moved across her shoulder blades. He wanted to touch them, wind them around his fingers. He bet they smelled like some kind of floral shampoo.

"No." Her answer was quiet in the stairwell. At the bottom she turned to look back at him, and he saw that the light had vanished from her eyes.

"Ah...mending a broken heart?" He backpedaled and changed his approach.

"Something like that." As she opened the door, her shoulders sagged a little, and Eddie followed, wanting to reach out a hand and comfort her.

* * *

"Pepperoni or mushroom?" Eddie asked as he opened the boxes. Steam poured out and wound its way upward.

Standing in the middle of the kitchen, Ash pulled the tops off two beer bottles. "Mushroom, please." She took a long swallow. "I'm a vegetarian."

"You're kidding."

"I'm not."

"You really don't eat meat?"

"I don't eat anything that used to have a face. It's just...I don't know. It makes me feel bad."

"How long?"

"Since college." She paused and sent a look straight through him. "Does it bother you?"

"Nah. Just never knew anyone like that before." Eddie separated the cheese as he pulled slices apart, two for each of them. "Napkins?"

Ash looked around. "I had some. I think Jen put them somewhere. Oh...on top of the fridge." She stood on tiptoes and reached for the unopened package. "What else do we need?"

"Nothing but a rooftop and some good conversation."

"Okay." She pulled open the window. "Here goes." She lifted one leg up and over the sill and hopped out. "The view's great out here."

He grabbed the rest of the six-pack, handed her the plates and followed. Wow. She was right. He walked to the railing that ran along the perimeter and surveyed the block from end to end. The trees laced together overhead, and he could smell the scent of flowers somewhere close by. Contentment settled over Eddie. He leaned against the side of the house and reached for the pizza.

Opposite him, a few feet away, Ash sat with her plate on her lap. Her shorts grazed the tops of her thighs, and through the thin skin of a gray T-shirt, Eddie could see small breasts punctuated with perfectly round nipples. He argued with the part of him that wanted to lose himself in the view and stopped looking. *Not going to do it, not now. She just broke up with her boyfriend. Give her a break.*

"So you and Jen went to school in the city?"

Ash nodded.

"College?"

"I was in law school. She just finished med school. We were both looking for a roommate a couple of years ago. Rest is history."

"You're kidding."

She smiled. "Nope."

He took a long pull on his beer. "Excuse me for asking, but what the hell are you doing in Paradise?" Shit, he felt about two feet tall next to someone who'd just finished becoming a lawyer. And that blonde – med school? Really? *Can't ever tell what's inside someone just by looking,* he reminded himself. *You should know that better than anyone.*

She gazed across the street. "I needed a change of scenery."

He laughed before he could help himself. "Well, you sure got one here. We're only a hundred miles from Boston, but it's a different world, in case you haven't noticed. Half the people in Paradise have never even been to Boston."

Ash's chin twitched, and she looked defensive. "Well, it seemed as good on the map as any other place. I just wanted to get away for awhile."

Eddie finished his slice and reached for another. "Don't get me wrong, it's a great town. Just don't see many city girls here, that's all." He paused. "So you going back in the fall? Got a job waiting for you?"

She shrugged a sort of yes. "Couple of my siblings are attorneys."

"Ah. Runs in the family?"

"I guess." Her voice dropped.

Eddie rested one wrist on his knee, dangling his empty bottle. "I gotta say, you don't sound very excited about it."

She sighed. "Ever since I was a little girl, I thought I knew exactly what I wanted to do. College, law school, work my way up to partner by the time I turn thirty, and then run for public office. Maybe end up in Congress."

Eddie stared, his mouth around a slice of pizza but forgetting to chew. Who the hell was this woman?

Ash went on as if the expression on his face hadn't changed in the least. "Turns out, that was more what my parents wanted me to do." She scratched her arm. "Truth is, I don't know what I want. I have a cousin who's running for office in the fall and can't wait for the fight." She grimaced. "But some things happened in the last couple of months that made me think twice about that. I don't think I'm cut out for a life in politics."

Eddie watched indecision trek across her forehead and down to the corners of her mouth. Law school grad or not, his housemate looked as uncertain about the future as half the people he knew. "You know, you don't have to decide your whole life tonight. Or even this summer."

"No? Tell that to my father."

"Ah, pressure from the parents." Eddie nodded.

"What about you? Did you always want to fix cars?"

"Oh, yeah." He cracked open another beer. "I was born for it. I've always known it. Used to drive my mom crazy, taking apart the vacuum cleaner, the lawn mower..." He chuckled and let the memories wash over him, good ones this time. "The minute I turned sixteen and bought my own beat-up Chevy, I knew what I wanted to do. It's like breathing to me." He leaned back. "Maybe I'll open my own shop someday, hire a couple of guys to work for me. That's all I'll need, that and a house with a garage big enough for three or four of my own."

"You really know what you want, huh?"

"Guess I'm lucky."

Ash didn't speak for a while after that, and Eddie wondered if he'd offended her somehow. He hoped not. He couldn't remember the last time he'd had a real conversation with a woman. He realized with surprise that he liked just talking to her, liked listening to her pause over her thoughts and choose her words instead of letting them spill from her mouth without meaning like so many other women he knew. Sitting up here near the trees, talking with someone who wasn't trying to impress him, felt good. For once, he wasn't thinking about how soon he could kiss her, or what would happen next. The now was all that mattered, talking to her and watching the color of her eyes change as she listened to him. He liked it.

Eddie let his eyes drift shut, basking in the leftover heat that still hung above them. Ever since The Accident he felt chilled, even in the warmth of summer. *The Accident.* He always thought of it spelled with capital letters, T.A., like B.C., which he guessed was sort of fitting, since it had split his life in two. Every memory he had was catalogued either Before The Accident or After The Accident.

Life without regret: Before The Accident. Staying out all night and going to work with a hangover the size of Colorado: Before The Accident. But after? Sleepless nights, aches that never ceased, and an enormous gulf between him and his parents. Even three years later, Eddie's ankles, and the scars on his face sometimes, throbbed in the cold weather. And the nightmares, of course, had stayed with him, once he'd finally been able to sleep at all.

He shook his head and swallowed deeply. Though he tried to will it away, a bright green light began to shine against the back of his eyelids, and his heart started its familiar racing. *Not here. Not now. For one day, I want to forget.* He swallowed again, but the racing continued, and shattered glass roared in his ears. He reached up and pinched the bridge of his nose. He counted to ten and tried to ignore the voices that screamed above the glass. No words, just voices lost in pain. *Ten. Eleven. Twelve. Please stop. Please.*

After a long minute, his heart slowed. The green light faded into the recesses of memory, and the agony of sound disappeared. His pulse returned to almost normal. Eddie dropped his hand back into his lap and opened his eyes.

Ash was staring at him.

"You okay?" Her voice, soft and low, crept across the porch. She didn't press, didn't ask him what was wrong, like people always did. Of course, she didn't know about the accident, and he figured she was about the only person in Paradise who didn't. Still, she didn't get nosy and pry. She just sat and studied him, concerned.

Eddie nodded and tried to find a smile. "Yeah. I'm fine." Yet a strange feeling of déjà vu raised the hairs on the back of his neck. His housemate, this person he'd just met, reminded him of someone he'd known years ago. He couldn't remember who. But he suddenly felt better than he had in a long, long time.

Chapter Four

Ash tucked the *Paradise Chronicle* under one arm and locked her door. She skipped down the steps and then paused for a minute in front of Eddie's apartment. Yesterday she'd passed it a few times as she carried the rest of her things upstairs, and it had only watched, a solid brown door with nothing but quiet behind it. Today, though, it studied Ash as she stood there. It hid possibilities, ones she wanted to know more about. *Maybe I should say hello. Say thanks for last night.* She raised her hand to knock.

He's different somehow. She thought Eddie West would be like most other good-looking guys she'd known, interested in himself and not much else. A memory of fraternity brothers tossing around a football and grilling on the quad during her undergrad days flashed into her mind. Eddie looked like a Sigma Chi, strong and masculine, the kind of guy who dated a different girl each week and won over his professors' hearts with a wink and a smile. Sigma Chi brothers didn't date girls like Ashton; they asked them for class notes or directions to the library. Then on Friday nights, they shared their drinks and their beds with blushing sorority girls or dark-eyed, mysterious graduate assistants who drank port and read Eliot.

Eddie had mentioned that he'd gone to tech school for a couple of years, opting to work on cars full-time as soon as he turned twenty. Okay, so he wasn't really like a Sigma Chi, not formally educated anyway. Still, there was something about him, something about the way he watched her with thoughtful eyes, that made Ash suspect he had more intellect and common sense than half the people she'd met at Harvard.

That's why I have to be careful, keep my distance. I can't let him find out who I am. I can't let anyone.

She let her hand drop away from his door. He'd probably gone to work, anyway. She hadn't heard him leave, but to her surprise she'd slept well, a long eight hours without waking once. Stepping onto the porch, she glanced down at the classified ads. She'd found three possibilities this morning and circled them in red ink, a declaration of her decision to stay in Paradise, at least for now. She'd figure out how to explain that to her parents when the time came.

"Waitress needed immediately for busy jazz club. Experience helpful but not necessary. Apply at Blues and Booze, 53 Main Street."

Paradise had a jazz club? A busy one? Ash smiled. She'd spent a couple of years sloshing coffee at the campus java joint; did that count as experience? She left her car at the curb and decided to walk. Three blocks later, the numbers on Main Street crept from forty-one, Lana's Plus Palace, to forty-five, a used bookstore, to forty-nine, Lou's Sub Shop. *Oh, right. Eddie mentioned this place last night.*

Ash slowed and peered into Lou's front window. A solitary cook in a stained white apron stood behind the counter, rolling dough. In front of him, a display case showed row upon row of deli meats, cheeses, and colorful salads. Her mouth watered, and she decided she'd stop by on her way back and pick up some lunch.

The sandwich shop sat on the corner of Adams Street, an alley barely wide enough for one car. Still, accustomed to busy Boston avenues, she glanced both ways before crossing it. On the other side, she found herself in front of a tall, narrow-fronted building with smoky windows. "Blues and Booze" read the neon sign above the door. She shaded her eyes. "Eleven to midnight," announced a paper sign in the window. Someone had scrawled "Help wanted" beside the hours.

She checked her watch and reached for the doorknob.

"Hello?" The word echoed in the space and fell away. To her right, a long bar stretched halfway across the room, ending at a curved doorway. Beyond the arch of the doorway opened another, larger room, draped in shadows. Chairs sat upside down on tabletops, skeletons in the darkness. At the far end of the restaurant she spied a thin strip of yellow underneath yet another door.

"Hello?" she called again and took a few more steps inside. This time the door in the dining room swung open, and a thin figure emerged.

"We're not open yet." A male voice, hoarse and curt, broke the stillness.

"Oh." She looked at her watch again. "I thought you opened at eleven."

The man walked toward her. Narrow-faced, with a chapped nose and black eyes, he peered at Ash and coughed. A navy blue apron was tied over wrinkled khaki pants and a flannel shirt with the sleeves rolled up. Yellow teeth crowded into a crooked row behind thin lips. Ash's stomach crawled into her throat, and she took a step backwards.

This was a mistake. Definitely a mistake. She wasn't cut out for a job in a place like this, a pampered girl from Boston's west side, and she knew it. Who was she kidding? She'd call home this afternoon and ask for money, deal with her parents' anger and disappointment somehow.

"Sorry," she said. "I'll come back later."

"No, wait," he said, and this time his voice was kinder. "You here for the job?"

She hesitated.

"Listen, you got any experience at all, you're hired. Hell, you don't got any experience, I'll probably hire you. Got no luck finding help in the summer when the college kids go home." He untied his apron and tossed it onto the bar. "So?" He pulled himself onto a barstool, lit a cigarette and waited.

Ash took one more look around and swallowed what little pride still hid in her heart. "Yes, I'm here about the job." She hoped he wouldn't try to shake her hand in hello. She could only imagine where his had been. Thankfully, he only nodded and blew a long stream of smoke toward the ceiling.

"Great. You ever work in a restaurant before?"

"Sort of. I worked behind the counter at a coffee shop for a couple of years."

The man took a long draw on his cigarette and considered. "Okay. What's your name?"

"Ashley Kirtland." It became a little easier, every day, to say the made-up name. "Ash." She hoped he wouldn't ask her for a reference. She could only ask Jen to lie for her so many times this week.

"Marty Evers. You want the job, come back at five tonight. I got another sorta-new girl, been here about two months. She'll show you the ropes." He sucked at the cigarette until it was a reddened stump between his fingers. "You available full time?"

Ash hadn't thought about that. Did she really want to spend forty hours a week in this place? "Days or nights?"

"Some of both. Course, you make more money at night. Tips ain't so good during the day."

"That's okay. Yeah, I'm available full time." What the hell. It would keep her mind off the messiness of the rest of her life.

"Good." Marty grabbed his apron and retreated back toward the kitchen. "Five o'clock," he repeated.

"Five o'clock," Ash agreed. She ran one finger along the dark wood of the bar. She needed a job. She needed to pay rent without asking her father for help or dipping into her trust fund. What difference did it make where she worked? It was only for a couple of months, anyway.

Your parents are going to kill you. Jen's words, as clear as if her best friend had walked into the bar and stood beside her, echoed inside Ash's conscience. It was true. A Kirk daughter, hauling trays of food around a seedy jazz club? She'd be the disgrace of the neighborhood if anyone found out back home. Well, maybe not. Her father had been filling that role the last few months. Not sure she could top his fiasco unless she started working the red light district.

Ash shook her head. That thought hurt, so she stopped it. Instead, she stepped into the sunshine and let the day cheer her.

* * *

A stop at Lou's for pasta salad and tomato soup, and Ash returned home. *Home.* The word sounded funny inside her head. She stood in the middle of her living room and looked around. Last night, after Eddie left, she'd laid out her faded but beloved Oriental rug and hung two Monet prints on the wall above the couch. Already the place looked better. Warmer. Another throw rug in the hallway, and it might actually feel like her own space.

She ventured into the kitchen and gazed out the window. Should she? The roof beckoned her, sun-dappled and secret. Jen had been right. The bird's eye porch was the best part of the apartment. Out there, she could escape. She could think. She could watch the world from above without it staring back at her. Ash grabbed a napkin along with her lunch and hauled herself across the sill.

The day was quiet, breathless in the heat. She watched the street for a while as she chewed, but nothing moved. Even Helen remained inside. Content for the first time in what seemed like forever, she allowed herself to relax.

God, she'd fallen apart when the news about her father broke. He'd tried to claim a set-up, a political framing, but how did you argue with the facts? A gram of cocaine in the glove box of his private Benz. A point-oh-nine on the breathalyzer test. Worst of all, a nineteen-year-old prostitute in the seat beside him, made up to look twenty-five but playing the lost little girl as soon as the first news camera appeared.

Her mother had defended him, as always. Ash finished her lunch and crumpled her napkin into a tiny ball. The space in the center of her chest ached. Was that what it meant to be a politician's wife? Smiling for the camera and denying any wrongdoing? Ash had no intention of letting that happen to her. Ever. She'd be the politician, but never the passive wife, never standing at home while her husband ran around behind her back.

Hell, now she didn't even want to be a politician. She'd spent her entire life watching how everyone, the people of Massachusetts, and the reporters themselves, had at first loved her father and then lambasted him. They worshipped him, put him into office with the biggest majority the state had seen in fifty years. And then they were the first ones to parade his mug shot across every television channel and newspaper in the city the moment he slipped up. Did she want a life like that for herself? No way.

Ash made her way back into the kitchen. She couldn't think about it anymore. The sorrow and frustration would give her a migraine and land her in bed for two days. With a couple of hours until she had to return to Blues and Booze, maybe she'd attack the mold growing behind her toilet. That chore might be disgusting enough to take her mind off all the problems back home.

Someone knocked on her door, and Ash froze. *Oh, God. They found me. The media followed me to Paradise and now they want a statement.* With a hearing scheduled for later this summer, the story would be building again, after the relative calm of the last few weeks. She eyed the door. She'd thought New Hampshire was far enough away, but who knew what those vultures were capable of? They'd camped outside her apartment in Cambridge until Colin called the police. Of course, that was when he'd still lived there. *When he still cared.* She hugged her elbows. All she wanted was to be left alone. Was that too much to ask?

She tiptoed to the door and looked through the peephole. *Eddie. Thank God.* She pulled open the door in relief.

"Hi."

Today her downstairs neighbor wore jeans and a faded red T-shirt with the words "Frank's Imports" across the pocket. His feet were bare. He lifted the edge of his shirt to wipe his forehead, and Ash caught a glimpse of a six-pack hiding underneath. Damn, he looked good. Even preoccupied with thoughts of her father, she couldn't deny that.

"Hi yourself. Everything okay?"

"Fine. Come on in."

"Thanks." A wide smile brightened his eyes, revealing a dimple.

God, he's even better-looking when he really smiles.

"How's the job search going?" He pointed to the paper, lying on the floor beside the loveseat.

"Ah, I found one." A vision of the darkened Blues and Booze flew into her mind, and Ash grimaced.

"Yeah? But that's not a good face."

"No, it's okay." She willed away the image of the manager's yellow teeth. "It's waiting tables in a restaurant downtown. Blues and Booze. You know it?"

"Sure. Great little place."

"Really?" She leaned in the kitchen doorway. "Seemed a little...I don't know. Strange."

He chuckled. "You probably talked to Marty, the manager."

She nodded.

"Marty's dad left him that place 'cause no one else in the family wanted it. He's got a sister who works in real estate down in Boston, and a brother out in California. Marty just made it through high school and didn't have the gumption to do much of anything. Actually, he's done all right for himself. That place always does a good business. Decent clientele. Any place on Main Street is safe enough, anyway. You don't need to worry about that."

Ash listened to him talk. She liked the way his mouth moved and the way his strong fingers rubbed a soft spot under his chin. "That makes me feel about a hundred times better. Thanks."

"When do you start?"

"Tonight. Five o'clock." A thought, brave enough to scare her, came from nowhere. "You should stop by."

He smiled but shook his head. "I'd like to, but I have to work the odd shift at the garage tonight. Three to ten. Frank stays open late one night a week." He looked at his watch. "I've got to get going. Just wanted to see how you made out."

"Oh, okay."

"But let me know how it goes. I'll stop by another time. Promise."

She nodded. "Sure. Have fun at work."

"Fun? Don't know about that." For a moment he stood in the doorway, and though neither one spoke, something bounced between them. Eyes met, then dropped, and Ash felt an orchestra of butterflies begin a symphony in her stomach. Eddie winked and headed out the door.

Ash sank to the floor and leaned against the loveseat. What was going on here? Somehow in the last twenty-four hours, Eddie West had slid into her life, smooth and easy as water winding its way down rocks on a lazy spring afternoon. She tried to decipher it, to understand the feeling of familiarity that emerged when they were together. It wasn't just attraction, though some of that hung over them too. It was almost as though they'd known each other a long time ago and were now trying to make up for all the years they'd been apart. She'd never sensed anything like it, and she wasn't sure how it made her feel.

She scratched her nose and wondered if it were possible to have a soul mate.

Chapter Five

A little after six the following night, Eddie eased his truck into an open spot on Main Street. He didn't bother to lock the doors. In Paradise, the last time anyone had something stolen in the daylight hours had been more than ten years ago. He ambled across the street to Blues and Booze. It had been a slow day at work, though he hadn't really minded. Some days he liked losing himself in the diagnostics, like figuring out why someone's alternator didn't work or why the idiot light on the panel kept blinking on and off.

But today, he'd appreciated the few oil changes and timing belts he'd had to take care of. Simple stuff. Nothing too complex. Because even though he'd done his best to concentrate, his mind kept going back to her. To Ash and to the few hours they spent having dinner the night before last.

Eddie pulled open the restaurant door and let his eyes adjust to the dimness for a moment before looking around. He'd been in here a few times as a teenager, maybe once or twice in the last couple of years. It used to be one of the only places in town you could drink without showing an ID. Not since Marty had taken over, though. Though not too bright in the business department, that guy only let himself get caught once for serving minors. Today the place catered more to the thirty-something and up crowd, though on any given day, schoolteachers, cabdrivers, and retired highway workers sat together at the bar watching a ball game.

"Jesus, that pitcher stinks," one of them said as he walked in. Eddie recognized Harold Triumph, former owner of Triumph Dry Cleaners, and pulled up a stool beside him.

"Draft, tall one," he said to the bartender.

"Hey! Eddie West!" The bartender grinned as he pulled on the tap. "Nick Scoles. Few years ahead of you back at Paradise High."

Eddie dropped a five on the bar. "Sure. How's it going?"

"Not bad. Got a couple-a new girls working here, so I'm enjoying the view."

A sharp sting of jealousy stiffened Eddie's spine. "I know. One of 'em's my housemate."

Nick started washing glasses. "Yeah? Which one?"

"Ash."

Nick nodded. "She's cute."

"Yeah she is." Eddie paused. "How's she doing, anyway?"

"Learning the ropes, I guess. Today's only her second day, so she hasn't screwed up too bad." He grinned around the toothpick in his mouth.

Eddie glanced over his shoulder in the direction of the dining room. Low-hanging lights cast shadows and made it hard for him to make out much of anything. A few tables were occupied, and a few more were covered with dishes and crumpled-up napkins. Near the door that led into the kitchen, two figures stood, filling water glasses and talking.

"Bathroom still in the same place?" Eddie asked.

Nick jerked one thumb toward the dining room. "All the way in the back."

Eddie ran one hand over his damp hair, smoothing it down. He was glad he'd stopped at the house to take a quick shower after finishing up at Frank's. He didn't want Ash to think he walked around smelling like diesel fumes all day. He headed into the dining room, taking his time. He passed one table with a young family he didn't recognize and another with a single man bent over a laptop, and slowed at a third when he recognized the two women having cocktails.

"Hey, Simra."

The bleach-blonde with the heavy eye makeup looked up. "Eddie?" She practically leapt out of her chair, dragging her napkin and menu with her. Flinging her arms around his neck, she leaned in for the squeeze.

Heavy perfume nearly choked him, and he pulled back after a minute. *Probably should've skipped the hello.* "How've you been?"

She leaned against the table, posing the way she used to back in high school. One hand on a hip and chin cocked up at him. Trouble was, her hair had grayed and her hips had broadened quite a bit in the last ten years, and the pose looked less come-hither and more tired-single-mother-aching-back. He wondered how many kids Simra was up to by now.

"How's Carl?"

She made a face. "Please. The loser left me last winter for a waitress over at the truck stop. Surprised you didn't hear about it."

Eddie was surprised too. News like that usually traveled through Paradise pretty quickly. Still, he'd been so wrapped up inside his own head the last few years that a train might have derailed and gone careening down Main Street without his noticing.

"Sorry to hear that." He cut a glance toward the kitchen door, where he thought he'd seen Ash a few minutes earlier.

"Oh, don't be." Simra reached over and tugged at Eddie's shirt. "That means you still have a chance."

His cheeks heated up. He'd gone on exactly one date with Simra Hall, five or six years ago, and the way she'd thrown herself at him in the back of his Camaro had turned him off fast. "I like women, but not when they don't let you do any of the catching," he told his buddies later on. "Shooting fish in a barrel isn't my style."

"This is Denise Reynolds. Lives over in Silver Creek." Simra turned to her friend, a redhead with graying roots, who gave Eddie a shy smile.

"Hi."

"Nice to meet you." Eddie nodded. "Listen, I'll catch up with you later. Nice seeing you."

"You, too." Simra leaned over and planted a kiss on his cheek before he could react. "Call me sometime. I'm staying with my parents over by the trailer park."

Eddie winked rather than answer and made a mental note to stay far away from the mobile home community until Paradise's grapevine told him Simra had gotten herself another man.

He continued through the dining room, waving a hand to Zach Olson and his wife, then stopped to drop a friendly kiss on the cheek of Mrs. Wainwright, his fifth grade teacher. Still, he hadn't caught sight of Ash and decided to head to the bathroom after all when the kitchen door swung open, and she nearly ran into him.

"Whoa!" Eddie took two steps back.

She backpedaled, and for a dangerous moment her tray tilted left. "Eddie?"

He reached over and helped her steady the steaming plates before they hit the floor. "Hi there."

Her face lit up, and he hoped it was because she was glad to see him and not just because he'd rescued the nachos and chicken fingers. Out of habit, he gave her a once-over, taking in her tight black shorts and the t-shirt that curved around her breasts and stretched the words "Blues and Booze" in just the right way.

"You here for dinner?"

"Just stopped by for a drink. And to say hello."

"Hey, sweetheart!" A burly guy Eddie didn't recognize waved a hand in the air. "You gonna bring us those nachos while they're still hot?"

"Sorry," Ash called over, and her cheeks pinked. "I gotta go."

"Yeah, okay."

"I'll come out and see you at the bar if I get a minute," she added.

"Hey, sweetheart!"

Eddie cut another glance across the room and didn't like what he saw: a middle-aged guy with red cheeks and bloodshot eyes, and two friends who looked in about the same condition. All three wore plaid shirts with the sleeves rolled up and expensive-looking watches. *They aren't locals.* They'd probably stopped in Paradise on business or signed up for a two-day seminar at the junior college.

"I'll see you later." Ash raised the tray above her head, winding her way through tables until she got to the three idiots.

He watched her go, backing toward the bathroom after a minute, though what he really wanted to do was stay and make sure those guys treated her okay. He didn't like the way they were looking at Ash, with grins splitting their faces apart and winks behind her back. As he watched, biting back a comment, they made her get them fresh napkins, fresh drinks, and extra plates before one of them finally ran a hand down her bare arm and let her go.

* * *

"So who's the guy?"

Ash looked up from the salads she was making. Lacey, the other waitress, stood with one hand on the coffee pot.

"What guy?"

The twenty-year old college student clicked her tongue. "C'mon. The one who just ran you over in the dining room. The one who was talking to you." She filled two mugs and headed for the door. "He's cute. Is he your boyfriend?"

"God, no. Just my housemate." Ash crooked her neck, trying to work out a kink. Thank goodness she was only working until eight. Already she'd had enough of drunken customers hitting on her to last through the summer.

"Cool. So is he available?"

Ash watched the young girl's eyes light up. She had to admit Eddie looked good in his polo shirt and shorts. Who wouldn't fall for those dimples, the hard body, that sensual voice? She straightened. Not her, that was for sure. It didn't matter how good Eddie West looked. She wasn't about to get involved with someone who lived downstairs from her. She'd learned that lesson in her first year of college.

"Ash?" Lacey stood in the doorway, waiting. "Do you know if he has a girlfriend?"

"Um... I don't know. I don't think so."

"What's his name?"

"Eddie West."

Lacey's brows flew up. "That's Eddie West? Geez, one of my roommates was talking about him the other day. Said she took her car in to get fixed and this gorgeous guy spent the afternoon hitting on her. Said she'd go out with him, too, if he ever called."

Ash laughed. "Did he?"

"No. I guess he's like that. You know, a player."

Ash swallowed. "Yeah? Could be. I really don't know him. I mean, we both just moved in..."

Lacey bumped the door open with one hip. "Well, I don't care. Guy looks like that, he can play with me all he wants." She laughed, a little chirp that hit Ash the wrong way.

Ash watched the door swing closed and returned to her salads. *See? That's one more reason you need to make sure you and Eddie stay just friends. He's already got a reputation a mile long. And if he's looking at you like...well, like he wants something more, remember that's what he does with any woman he meets.*

She took another couple of minutes, hoping Eddie had made it back to the bar, before she headed into the dining room.

"Hey, sweetheart!"

Ash stiffened. When were those guys going to leave? Did they have any idea who she was? Who her father was? She pressed her lips together and turned around.

"Can I get you something else?"

One of them, the heaviest, ran his tongue over his bottom lip. "Sure can."

How about the check? she almost said as she made her way over to their table.

Before she could stop him, the guy wrapped one arm around her waist and yanked her into him. "How about you give me your phone number, good-lookin'?"

Ash's hipbone pressed into the spongy flesh of his belly as she tried to pull away. "Um, listen..."

"C'mon. Sweet little thing like you probably tastes even better than she looks." The other two guys at the table guffawed. "What time do you get off?"

Ash shoved a palm against his shoulder. "Let go of me."

But he wouldn't. "What's wrong? You got a boyfriend or something?"

"No, but – "

"Take your hands off her."

The voice, low and angry, came from behind her. Startled, the guy unwrapped himself from her waist, and she almost fell into Eddie in her rush to get away. He put one hand on her shoulder, and her legs turned wobbly with relief.

"You okay?" he breathed into her ear.

A tingle ran down her arm. *Uh-oh.* Tingles weren't good. Well, they were, but not in this case. She wasn't supposed to let her neighbor knock her off her feet with desire. Ash took a step back to catch her balance and nodded. Eddie glared at the guys, who'd turned back to their nachos with sheepish faces. He lowered his voice another degree, so that his next words came out as a clear threat.

"You touch her again, you even breathe wrong when you're asking for a glass of water, I'll make sure you don't walk straight for the next week."

"Whatever," one of them muttered.

Eddie strode over to the table. Biceps flexed as he put both hands on the back of an empty chair and squeezed. "What'd you say?"

"Nothing, man," one of the other guys said. "We're leaving anyway."

"Good idea."

And as Ash watched, Eddie stood there with arms crossed as she brought them the bill and collected their tab, plus an extra twenty for her tip.

"You didn't have to do that."

He shrugged, the angry look melting away as the three finally stumbled out of the restaurant. "They were being assholes."

She walked over to him, thankful down to the tips of her toes. Without letting herself think too much about it, she planted a kiss on Eddie's scarred cheek. "Thank you."

"Ah, it wasn't anything." But he didn't move and neither did she, until a crowd of people came into the restaurant and she had to help Lacey with the order. The next time Ash checked the bar, Eddie was gone.

Chapter Six

The following week, Ash dragged herself back to Lycian Street after a hectic lunch shift. A toddler had managed to spill iced tea down her legs, and her right sock had turned a strange yellow color. Her arms ached. Her legs ached. And it was only four o'clock in the afternoon. Thank God she had tomorrow off.

The sun beat down on a mid-June day that felt more like the heaviness of August. She checked her cell phone. Her mother had called once in the last week, leaving a teary message that pleaded with Ash to return to Boston.

"We need the whole family together," Mamie Kirk wept on the voicemail. "Please, Ashton. Your father needs to know we all support him."

But did they? Ash didn't know what to believe. She didn't know who was telling the truth and who was making up tales. She slowed as she passed Lou's and breathed in the aroma of fresh bread and garlic. Two cars drove by. A mother with her baby in a stroller jogged down the sidewalk. The church clock chimed the hour.

The muscles in her neck unclenched, and her fatigue eased. *It's so different from Boston,* she thought for the umpteenth time. True, Paradise had only one grocery store, no movie theater, and no Wal-Mart. It had a single stoplight that turned to blinking yellow after midnight. It did have a train station, but it seemed as though more people left the town than returned to it. It sat shrouded by low mountains, a stone's throw from one of the largest cities in the country, and yet sometimes Ash felt as though she couldn't have been more protected, more isolated, than if she'd moved to the moon.

"It's nice," she said aloud. *And I don't want to go back to Boston. Not now. Not yet.* She just had to figure out how to explain that to her mother.

Reaching her street, Ash turned the corner and dug into her pocket for her keys. After a hot shower, maybe she'd see if Eddie was in the mood for some Chinese food. Though they hadn't seen too much of each other in the last few days, she'd heard him down there, blasting his rock music and rearranging furniture. Since moving in three weeks ago, they'd shared a couple of early dinners and a beer or two on the porch. Other than that, their paths didn't cross too often. Still, she liked knowing he was there. It made the house a little more full, the nights a little less lonely, when she curled into bed and tried not to dream of Colin.

A breath of air moved around the corner, blowing strands of hair that had fallen from her ponytail. The weekend stretched out ahead of her without so much as a single lunch shift to keep her busy. Anxiety bubbled inside her chest. She needed something to keep her mind off her mother's calls. Off her father's predicament. Off the heartache that wouldn't go away.

Man, she hoped Eddie was home. She hoped he didn't have plans for dinner.

"Hey, stranger."

He sat on the front porch, a six-pack between his feet and a lazy grin on his face.

"Hey, yourself." She smiled and dropped to sit on the top step. "You're home early."

"Yeah. Frank's going outta town for the weekend, closed at two." He flipped the top off a bottle and handed it over.

"Thanks. How'd you know that's exactly what I need?"

Eddie took a long pull on his own bottle. "Figured you'd be pretty beat. Fridays always get a big lunch crowd down at the restaurant."

Ash cocked one eyebrow. "Thanks for giving me a heads-up. You could have let me know." She leaned against the porch railing. Nothing moved. No cars turned down their block. No joggers ran by; no kids played in the park across the street. She closed her eyes and welcomed the silence.

"So how was work this week?" she asked after a while.

"Same as always. Crazy customers want to know why we can't fix their cars in an hour, when they've been driving around for two weeks with the problem."

Ash smiled. "Yeah, people are funny that way."

"So what's for dinner?"

She turned. "Whatever you're making."

He laughed, and she noticed that his goatee had grown a little more in the last few days. Thick and dark, it caught the light and turned a reddish-brown in places. *Not like Colin or anyone else I ever dated.* All her past boyfriends had smooth faces and baby-soft cheeks. For the first time, she realized she liked the look of stubble on a man. Hot. Rugged. Rough in all the right ways.

She dropped her chin, hoping Eddie couldn't read her thoughts. "I was thinking about ordering Chinese."

"Sounds good to me."

"You don't have plans for tonight? It's Friday. "

"Nope."

"No hot dates?"

"Not until tomorrow."

"Oh." Ash studied the stain on her sock. With one hand, she reached up and loosened her ponytail, damp with perspiration. "Who's the lucky girl?"

Eddie cleared his throat. "Cheri Ryerson." Long pause. "Don't think you know her."

Ash got up, sticking her empty bottle back inside the cardboard carrier. "Don't think I do. She live in Paradise?"

"Next town over."

"Well, lover boy, I'm sure you'll have a good time."

He stood too, following her to the door. "I'm sure I will."

They were halfway inside when Helen called to them from across the street. Ash had one hand on the doorknob, and Eddie was picking up the empties, when the woman hobbled over.

"Ashley!" Helen's voice scratched on the syllables, and her breathing came in great gasps. "Edward!"

In slow motion, Ash turned. She didn't like the tone in the woman's voice: eager, gossipy, dangerous. She took a step back, meaning to create some sort of excuse and head upstairs. But Eddie had already loped down the steps, a playboy grin on his face.

Helen stopped in the middle of the sidewalk, hands on her hips. "I was downtown today, getting my hair done." She stopped, drawing in a deep, rattling breath. "And a newspaper reporter came into Hair Heaven. From Boston."

Oh, God. Ash took two steps across the porch and tumbled down the stairs, straight into Eddie's back. Into Eddie's strong, tall, incredibly muscular back. He turned and grabbed her with both hands before she knocked the two of them over.

"You okay?"

She blew out a long breath, conscious of his hands on her even as she looked at her feet and willed Helen away. "I'm fine. Just tired. Sorry."

The white-haired woman looked as though she hadn't even noticed. "He was asking about someone named Ashton Kirk." Her beady eyes stared at Ash. "I told him I'd never heard of anyone by that name."

Eddie shrugged. "Guess it sounds a little like Ash's name, but – "

"But it's not," Ash finished.

"Of course it's not." He let his arm drop around Ash's neck, looping it across her shoulders. "Why was he all the way up here, anyway?"

Helen pulled a crumpled tissue from her pocket and blew her nose. "I don't know. Said he was looking for Senator's Kirk's daughter."

"In Paradise?" Eddie began to laugh. "Why? Don't those types stay close to home?"

Something like a stone sank inside Ash. *Those types...*

"That's what I told him," Helen said. "Said there wasn't any reason for a stuck-up politician's daughter to get her hands dirty way up here in New Hampshire. I guess he had some kind of lead. Thought maybe she skipped town to get away from the family mess."

"Can't say I'd blame her." Eddie turned to Ash. "You don't know who she's talking about, do you? You ever meet the senator's daughter?"

The stone got larger and threatened to lodge itself in Ash's throat. She managed to shake her head.

"Guess he's out of luck," Eddie said.

Helen reached into the pocket of her dress and pulled out a business card. "Here. He passed them around to everyone who was in the salon, said to call if we had any information. I figure you have more chance of meeting someone like that than I do." She handed the card to Eddie, who stuck it in the back pocket of his shorts. Ash caught herself looking at the smooth, tanned strip of skin along his lower back as his shirt pulled up and ordered herself to stop it, once and for all.

"Thanks, Helen," Eddie said. "I'll let you know if I hear anything."

"Well, I hope so," the woman went on. "Sadie said she wouldn't believe it, if a daughter of..."

Ash barely heard the words. *It's only a matter of time before someone finds out.* She backed away and let Eddie's arm drop, missing its heaviness when she did. *What am I doing? How the hell did I think I could get away with this?*

Chapter Seven

Sunday morning, Ash awoke to the sound of rain drumming the rooftop. *Great.* She'd planned on checking out the antique shops over in Silver Creek that afternoon. She rolled over and pushed her face into her pillow. Somehow, the idea of tromping through puddles on her way to and from the car didn't appeal. She eyed the clock. Six a.m. Gray light filtered through the curtains. It curled into the corners of the bedroom and draped itself around her shoulders. *No reason to get up,* she thought, slipping back into sleep. *No reason at all.*

As she moved back toward dreams, she wondered if the rain would clear later on. Eddie had promised to come up and watch the baseball game with her, explain once and for all why the Red Sox southpaw was the league's best pitcher in twenty years. If the lousy weather postponed the opening pitch, she'd likely be stuck watching Lifetime movies or Seinfeld reruns by herself.

"The Sox are playing the Yankees this weekend," he'd told her Friday, over chicken lo mein (his) and tofu with seaweed (hers). "I'll stop up on Sunday and show you how a real baseball fan watches the game."

"You do that," she answered, smiling at him as they counted fireflies from the rooftop. "You do that..."

* * *

The next sound Ash heard was a slam. Then a shout. She sat straight up in bed and stared at the clock. Quarter to eleven. Rain still poured down, pattering against the windows. She reached for her robe and listened for the sound that had pulled her from sleep. Nothing for a minute. Then it came again: a series of thumps, followed by a male voice swearing. Eddie's voice. Ash swung her feet over the edge of the bed and rubbed her eyes.

What the hell is going on down there?

Now it sounded like he was running in circles around his apartment. *Is he working out? Doing laps instead of going to the gym?* Ash made her way to the kitchen and turned on the coffee pot. She knew the guy kept himself in shape, but in his own apartment? On a Sunday morning?

His date. He's with his date from last night, that woman from Silver Creek. Cheri something. Ash's cheeks warmed. Of course. They were probably playing some kind of silly morning-after game, running half naked around his apartment while she winked and squealed and played hard to get. Before Ash could stop herself, the vision slipped inside her mind's eye: Eddie, wearing nothing but a pair of boxer shorts, catching the girl with those strong hands. Pulling her close and rubbing gentle thumbs along bare shoulders before leaning in for a kiss. A long kiss. A kiss that began in the hallway and ended somewhere in a tangle of sheets.

Ash pinched the skin on one arm to make herself stop. *Don't think about Eddie that way.* She pulled her hair into a ponytail and poured herself a steaming mug of coffee. She doused it with cream and took a long sip, not caring that it burned her tongue. *You're just friends, remember? Just neighbors, two people who share a house. It doesn't matter who he spend his nights with. Or his mornings.*

So why did the thought make her so damned uncomfortable?

Another crash. Ash jumped in her chair. Damn. So the guy had company last night. He didn't have to rub it in. She finished her coffee and shoved the mug away. Well, she might as well shower and find something to do with her day. No use sitting here, listening to Mr. Hotshot Lover chase his latest conquest around the bed.

She wrapped her robe around her and was heading into the bathroom when a knock landed on her door.

"Ash?"

She froze. *You've got to be kidding me.* What, did her want her to play referee?

He knocked again, louder and longer. "Ash? You in there?"

Oh, for Christ's sake. She was in no mood. She marched to the door and yanked it open. "What do you want?"

Eddie stood in the hallway, a hangdog look on his face. By himself. Ash peered over his shoulder. No model-thin woman hovered behind him. No scent of leftover perfume hung in the air, either. Ash narrowed her eyes. "What's going on?"

Eddie raked his fingers through his hair, making it stand on end. Barefoot, he wore a pair of frayed sweats, cut off at the knees, and an old Patriots jersey with the sleeves torn off. A fuzz of pillowcase was stuck to his chin, and Ash had to pin her arms to her sides to keep from reaching up to brush it away.

"Can you help me?"

"With what? Sounds like you're starting up a circus down there."

"No, it's..." He glanced over his shoulder, and worry wrinkled his face. When he looked back at her again, she thought she might fall right inside those eyes, those pools of blue, and not come up for a week.

"I found a kitten." He ducked his chin. "Outside."

"A what?"

"A kitten. A really small one. It was hanging around last night, and then when I went out to get the paper this morning it was still there, sitting in the middle of the sidewalk. Soaking wet."

"So you brought it inside?" Ash began to smile. Not a woman after all down there. Just a scared fluff of fur that her strapping, six-foot neighbor had decided to bring in out of the storm. Oh, hell. She was already halfway to falling for this guy. Now he had to turn into a total softy on her?

Eddie shrugged. "Well, it was sort of...limping around. And crying. And I thought if I left it out there I'd be about the worst person in the entire world, so..."

Ash took one step into the hallway. "And now you can't catch it."

"Yeah. Thought I'd keep it in the bathroom, but it got out."

"Come on." She pushed past Eddie and made her way down the stairs barefoot. She was standing in front of his door before she considered if she should have changed into something more substantial than a cotton robe that barely came to her knees.

"I think he's under the chair," Eddie said. As they walked inside, he pointed to a leather recliner in the corner.

Ash tiptoed over and kneeled down, wondering if the breeze on the backs of her thighs meant her robe wasn't covering much. She readjusted. "I don't see anything."

"Well..." Eddie turned in a slow circle. "I closed the door. He couldn't have gotten far."

Ash pushed herself back up and leaned over a blue corduroy sofa with its tags still attached. A dust ball danced across the hardwood, but no cat. She looked under the end table, and behind Eddie's entertainment center, which took up half the living room with its enormous television.

Nothing.

"Maybe in the bedroom?" She felt funny looking in there.

"Maybe." Eddie strode past her down the hall. He whistled under his breath, a meek little coaxing tune that made her smile.

Ash hung back and watched as he looked in the corners of his sparsely furnished bedroom. *This place could definitely use a woman's touch.* Someone had hung navy blue curtains on the windows, but otherwise the walls remained bare. A desk and matching chair were the only other pieces of furniture she could see, besides the box spring and mattress lying on the floor. A queen size, she noticed, not too big and not too narrow. Really, just the perfect size for two people to curl up in.

"Ash?" Eddie waved a hand in front of her face. "You still there? Thought you were gonna help me look."

"Oh. Sorry." She glanced around at a faint meow. Eddie cocked his head. The meow came again. "Bathroom." In an instant, he had darted past Ash, and a moment later he emerged holding a soggy ball of black and white. "Got him."

"Wow. It is small."

A rumble started up in the kitten's throat.

"I told you." Eddie peered down at it.

Ash took hold of one of the kitten's legs and pushed aside damp fur. "There's a cut here. A bad one. No wonder it's limping." She lifted a towel off the rack inside the bathroom door and wrapped it around the animal. "Here." In a moment she had clutched it to her chest, nuzzling it and blotting off the worst of the water. "Might want to get it to a vet. Know anyone who's open on Sundays?"

"Maybe." Eddie loped off into the kitchen and re-emerged a moment later, cell phone in hand.

Ash returned to the living room and sat on the couch, kitten in her lap. Bright green eyes looked up at her, and a weak mew escaped its pink mouth. A tiny paw batted at the finger she reached out to it. She grinned. The only pet she and Colin ever had was Buster, the oversized goldfish. She used to watch him swim circles in his stupid glass bowl and wish for just a day that her boyfriend wasn't deathly allergic to all things furry.

"Now I don't have to worry about that, do I?" she murmured into the cat's head.

"Ash?" Eddie appeared in the doorway. "Friend of mine in Tompkins Heights'll take a look at it this afternoon."

"Really?" Ash looked up, suddenly aware of the way her robe fell apart at the neck and her bare legs stretched down to the hardwood floor. As she watched, he dropped a glance to her toenails—newly painted red, as of last night in front of the TV—before turning a shade of crimson himself.

"Anyway, thanks for the help."

"No problem." She paused. "You know, I wasn't sure what was going on down here. Thought maybe you were still entertaining your date from last night."

"Cheri?" He chuckled. "Nah."

"Things didn't work out?"

"We had a good time. But she wanted to come in, stay a while, and..." He shrugged.

"You didn't?"

"Woman stays the night, things get complicated."

Ash nodded, fingers stroking the kitten's fur as its purr regulated into a steady rhythm. "And you don't like things to be complicated."

"Do you?"

Ash shook her head. *No*, she answered silently. *They're complicated enough already.*

Chapter Eight

"Ash!" Marty stuck his head into the kitchen of Blues and Booze.

She pulled her tips from her pocket and started to count. "What's up?" It had been a long week, and she couldn't wait for the night to be over. Thank God the clock read ten minutes to twelve.

"Some guy out here says he knows you." The manager wheezed. One arm snaked up to scratch an itch between his shoulder blades. He peered into the coffee pot, pulled some brown strands of lettuce from the salad bin, and straightened the cocktail napkins.

Ash's shoulders hunched up, and she didn't answer for a minute. *The media? No. Not at almost midnight.* But she knew better than anyone that the paparazzi didn't watch the clock.

"You hear me?"

"I heard you. Who is he?"

"Dunno. He's got a couple of tattoos. Says his name's Eddie something."

Coins slipped through her fingers like water. "Oh. Yeah, he knows me. Tell him I'll be right out." She bent to retrieve quarters from the sticky floor and waited for Marty to leave. She'd only seen Eddie twice in passing, the last couple of days. Both times he'd paused, placed a hand on her shoulder, and smiled down at her like there was nowhere else he wanted to be. The gesture made her uncomfortable as hell. It made her look forward to walking down the stairs each morning. It made her wonder who had taken over her body and replaced her with a woman who grew warm and slippery every time she saw this guy. A guy she barely knew.

Watch it, Ash, she warned herself for the tenth time since moving to Paradise. *Falling for this guy is trouble.* Wrapping her apron into a ball, she admitted that as much as she wanted to avoid complications, she was still glad Eddie had come to see her tonight. She wanted to ask him how the kitten was making out. She wanted to tell him about the idiot who'd grabbed at her earlier and laugh with him about the woman who'd sent her meal back three times before ordering something else altogether. Mostly, Ash wanted Eddie to drop an arm across her shoulders or rub a hand across the top of her head and tell her she was doing okay.

He sat alone in the bar, on the stool closest to the door. An empty beer mug stood in front of him, with a few crumpled dollar bills beside it. Ash paused for a minute in the dining room and peered through the chair legs, now perched upside down on their tables.

J.T., one of the night bartenders, leaned on his elbows and told a joke out of one side of his mouth. Ash watched Eddie listen, watched the scars in his cheek dip and crease when he laughed, and she wondered again where the scars had come from, and why he hadn't erased them. The one along his jawline, especially, cut so deep that surely plastic surgery could have softened it. Had he tried it? Had the surgery failed? She wiped her palms on her shorts. She knew nothing about Eddie and his scars, not really. Maybe he'd been born with them. Maybe they reminded him of something he didn't want to forget. Maybe he didn't want softening.

She crossed the floor and snuck up beside him. "Hi there."

Eddie smiled and gave her a soft punch on the arm. "Hi, yourself. Done for the night?"

"Yeah. Finally."

"You getting used to it?"

"I guess. Honestly, it's harder than I thought." That, at least, was true. Ash had no idea her feet could ache so, or that her legs could turn wobbly after a night of running trays back and forth. In just a couple of weeks, she'd discovered a newfound appreciation for the people who did it day in and out, year after year. She knew she could never be one of them, dependent upon tips to pay a mortgage, cover car insurance, or put food on the table.

J.T. flipped on the television as he wiped down the bar. Ash tensed. *Not the news, please.* She eyed the clock. Just about midnight. Good. Maybe the highlights would be through. She didn't need any news from Boston discussing the senator's latest statement or the opposing attorney's trial preparations. She fidgeted on the stool beside Eddie and sipped a glass of water.

"I should get going," she said. She watched the screen and prayed no political report would appear. "I'm beat."

"You drive tonight?" Eddie didn't look at her, just asked the question sideways as he watched a preview for some new reality show.

"Um, yeah." She always drove when she worked the night shift. Didn't matter that everyone she'd met told her she could walk down Main Street at two in the morning and not see a soul. City habits didn't die that quickly. She'd keep on driving herself, for a while anyway. Until Paradise seeped into her veins a little more.

"Okay if I catch a ride back with you?" he asked. "I walked."

This time he did turn toward her, and his gaze landed on her with such intensity that she felt as though he'd burned right through the fabric of her shirt.

"Ah, sure." *Stop doing that to me. Stop setting me on fire every time I get too close to you.* "How's the cat?" she asked, to change the subject.

"Better. Vet gave it some antibiotics."

"You keeping it?"

He shrugged. "Haven't decided yet."

J.T. adjusted the volume, turning it up as the final highlights from the eleven o'clock news flashed across the screen.

"Tomorrow at six," the chipper blonde anchor announced, "tune in for the latest chapter in the Senator Kirk arrest."

Ash's throat closed.

"We'll hear from the woman who used to work as the Kirks' personal housekeeper, as well as tell you what's in store for this sullied senator from Boston..."

Ash set her glass down on the bar, too hard. A crack splintered all the way up one side.

J.T. frowned. "Geez, take it easy. You okay?"

"Sorry. Wasn't paying attention, I guess."

He swept it into the trash. "No biggie. It happens."

Ash buried her hands between her legs so Eddie wouldn't see them tremble.

"Can you believe that guy?" he said, still staring at the TV. "You'd think we could find one honest politician somewhere in the whole damn country. But no. Even the ones who come across as Mr. Family Man, who tell us they're gonna change things for the better—"

"Yep," J.T. agreed, cutting him off. "Even they wind up bein' like all the rest. Making decisions from between their legs. Kirk's no better. Another John fuckin' Kennedy." He pulled on the tap and poured Eddie another beer.

Ash cleared her throat. "You know, some people say maybe he's innocent. That he was set up by someone who didn't want him to get the vice-presidential nomination."

Eddie chuckled. "Yeah, sure. They're all innocent. Like JFK. And Jefferson, sleeping with his slaves."

"Don't forget Bill Clinton," J.T. added.

Eddie laughed out loud. "Oh, yeah. Especially Clinton. He was the most innocent of all. He and Kirk are probably buddies. Probably sit around over stogies and talk about the best blow jobs they ever got."

Ash stiffened. "It could be true," she said. "The setup, I mean."

Eddie turned. "Kirk was busted DUI. Caught with coke and a hooker. How the hell does someone set that up?"

She didn't know. She'd been asking herself the same question every night since the arrest. But if her father said he was framed, then part of her, the little-girl part that still remembered the way he'd sung her to sleep every night as a child, had to hold out hope.

"Maybe the Republicans held him down and poured whiskey down his throat," J.T. offered and snorted as he laughed at his own joke.

"Yeah, and maybe they forced him into the car at gunpoint with that hot little piece of tail," Eddie continued. He tipped his head back and took a long drink.

"Did they ever say whether his zipper was up or down when the cops pulled him over?"

Ash slid off her stool. "You ready to go?"

"Hang on. Let me finish my beer."

"I'm ready now."

Eddie's jaw twitched. "Can't you give me five minutes? What's wrong with you?"

She crossed her arms and shifted from foot to foot. "I'm tired, okay? That's what's wrong with me. My feet feel like they're going to fall off, I smell like ketchup, and I'm about sick to death of listening to the two of you rip apart some guy you don't even know. Half of what the media reports isn't even true. More than half."

She stopped to draw a breath, and silence echoed through the bar. J.T. whistled, long and low. Eddie frowned, and something dark slid across his face.

"You know, I think I'll walk after all," he said after a long minute of staring at her. "Could use some fresh air." He shoved some bills across the bar, scraped his stool out of the way, and headed for the door. "Thanks, J.T.," he said. The door slammed shut behind him.

Ash watched Eddie's shadow disappear down the block. Well, fine. She hadn't wanted to drive home with him, anyway. She tried to believe her own lie as she walked to her car in silence a few minutes later. One flickering motion light clicked on as she crossed the back parking lot. Her VW started up with a hesitation, a little cough before catching, and she crossed her fingers that it would turn over.

Probably should get it looked at. She dropped her forehead onto the steering wheel. But where? By who? The only repair shop she knew of in Paradise was the place Eddie worked, and now she couldn't take it there. Suddenly, she felt lonelier than the day Colin had left her.

Ash sighed. She hadn't meant to say those things, hadn't meant to lose her temper. She just couldn't help it sometimes. Not for the first time, she thought she'd probably make a lousy courtroom lawyer. Holding her tongue wasn't her strong suit. She bumped her way out of the parking lot and turned onto Spruce Street, taking the long way home.

She was better off anyway, keeping her distance from Eddie. Keeping her distance from all of them. She didn't need to listen to him or anyone else say things like that about her father. Randolph Kirk had screwed up, but he was still Ash's blood. Her fingers tightened around the steering wheel as she passed the silent town square and eased through the intersection in the center of town. A lonely yellow eye blinked down at her.

But why did you do it, Dad? Even if someone had set him up, even if someone planted the drugs and spiked his drink, what was he doing in a car with a girl younger than his own daughters? Tears started up, and as Ash made her way back to Lycian Street, she braked hard and edged to the curb. She didn't know. She couldn't find the answers. And she didn't trust herself to ask her father.

She looked up and saw a dark house. If Eddie was home, he'd turned off all the lights, even the porch one they always kept burning. Now it looked like all the other buildings on the block: lifeless and cold. She raised both hands to her face and wept.

Chapter Nine

Ash balanced a grocery bag in the crook of each arm and propped open the front door. She blew her bangs off her forehead. Where was the mild summer the weatherman had promised back in May? Each day in Paradise, she'd woken to nothing but humid temperatures that hovered around ninety. No rain, no relief, just heat and heaviness pouring down from above. At only noon on a Saturday, she'd already soaked through a T-shirt on her way back from the store.

"Ugh." She let the bags slide to the floor and checked her mailbox. She'd worked well past midnight last night, thanks to a lively crowd that kept the band playing long after regular closing. She really couldn't complain, though, not with a pocket full of tips that totaled well over a hundred dollars.

Someone giggled.

Ash closed the rusted door to her mailbox and spun around. She frowned. No one on the porch. No gaggle of pre-teen girls walking along the sidewalk. She heard it again: a giggle, definitely feminine. Turning in a slow circle, she eyed Eddie's door.

"Woman stays the night, things get complicated..."

She swallowed. Looked as though Eddie had set himself up for some complications after all. She negotiated the paper bags back into her arms, wanting to get upstairs as quickly as she could. Sure, her housemate was entitled to entertain whoever he wanted, whenever he wanted, but that didn't mean she had any interest in seeing who it might be. They hadn't spoken since that night in the bar, and she'd done her best to keep it that way. What would she say to him, anyway?

Ash turned away, but not quickly enough. Eddie's door opened, and a petite blonde stepped into the foyer. Eddie followed. At their feet trotted the kitten, batting at the blonde's heels.

"Y'all are too much," she said, with a nudge at Eddie's chest. "I don't believe a single thing you say." The words floated on the air, laced with a southern accent. Her mouth crinkled up at the edges as she laughed. Eddie scooped up the kitten and, with a rough pet across the top of its head, steered it back inside his apartment. The moment he shut his door, though, it began to cry, in plaintive little mews that broke Ash's heart.

She stared at a patch of wall behind Eddie's head, one knee propped under a grocery bag that had begun to seep something sticky.

"Oh, hi," the blonde said. "I didn't see you standing there."

Ash felt her grip loosening. "Hi."

"I'm Savannah," she added.

Ash fought back a smile. Savannah? Did people really name their children such things? Yet somehow it fit this model-thin woman standing in the entryway, smelling like Eddie's soap and flushed with morning lovemaking. Her fingers threw long, thin shadows on the walls as she adjusted her ponytail, like anemone waving in ocean breezes. Ash looked down at her own knotty knuckles and wondered if Eddie noticed hands as much as she did.

"Ash," she said after a minute. "I live upstairs."

"Oh." The blonde's eyes widened. "You're the lawyer, right?"

Ash shot Eddie a look. He'd told his bed bunny about her? While something about that pleased her, down deep where she didn't dare analyze it, she didn't need too many people knowing about her past. Least of all someone who probably chattered to half of Paradise on a daily basis. Ash should have known better.

She should have kept it all to herself, every last detail. It was just safer that way.

"Well, sort of. I haven't passed the bar exam yet."

Savannah shook her head. "Wow. I couldn't even make it through two semesters at JC. Too boring."

Ash's back began to ache. She glanced at Eddie. *Say something. Don't just stand there.* But he didn't. Not to her, anyway. He just put his arm around Savannah's waist after a minute and led her out into the morning.

Ash watched them go, and jealousy sparked a hot stone in her stomach. *That's what he likes? A ditzy bottle-blonde who barely made it out of high school?* She slid to a seat, knees rubbery. Raspberry jelly had leaked through one bag, gluing her shorts to her legs. She rubbed her temples and told herself not to care.

She'd barely had a half-dozen conversations with him. He wasn't her type, anyway. He spent two years in college. She went to Harvard. He spent his life in Paradise, and she was using it as a place to hide out. He dated a different woman each week. She was trying to get over a three-year relationship. He fixed cars, and she —what, Ash? What exactly are you going to do with yourself now that you've decided that a hundred-thousand dollar degree isn't going to work out the way you'd planned?

As if on cue, her cell began to ring.

Ash pulled the phone out of her pocket and checked the screen. Her oldest sister. Terrific.

"Hello?"

"Ashton? Where are you?" Jessica Kirk-Malloy's voice, no-nonsense and demanding an answer, spat through the receiver.

"What do you mean, where am I?"

"Don't play stupid. I know you moved out of your apartment. I saw Colin last week." She paused, and the edges of her words softened a little. "I didn't know you two broke up. Sorry."

Like you really care. "Yeah, well, things weren't working out."

"Mm hmm." Jess paused. "So what happened? Dad knows you turned down the job at Deacon and Mathers, by the way. He's furious. You know he went to school with Bill Mathers, right?"

Of course she knew. It was all he'd talked about after they offered her the position. It was the other, unspoken, reason Ash hadn't felt right about taking it. She wanted to prove herself after law school, make it on her own. Finding out her father had pulled strings had soured her on the whole deal.

"Mom says you've been avoiding her calls."

"I haven't been avoiding them. She just calls when I'm sleeping. Or working."

"So you can't call her back?"

"And say what?" Ash exploded. "How's life on the home front? Is Dad ready for the hearing? Tell me, Jess, did he call in another favor to avoid jail time, or is that the next headline I'm going to read when I pick up the paper?"

"Don't be cruel."

What am I supposed to be, then? The good little daughter, who stands by her family no matter what?

"When are you coming home?" Jess tried another line of questioning.

"I'm not."

Pause. "What does that mean?"

Ash rubbed at the stain on her shorts. Her fingers came away red. "It means I'm taking some time off this summer, okay? Yeah, I left Boston for a while. To get my head straight. Sorry if you and Anne have to handle the media circus by yourselves. But I can't do it anymore. I just can't." To her surprise, Ash began to cry. Little choking noises broke from her lips.

Jess didn't say anything.

"Don't tell Mom and Dad, please?"

"What am I supposed to say when they ask?"

"That I'm subletting an apartment for the summer."

"Where?"

"New Hampshire." It was as much as she could say.

"New—" Jess sputtered for a minute and then ran out of steam. "Fine. I'll do my best to lie for you." The guilt stabbed Ash right where she knew her sister meant it to.

Jess sighed. "You're sure you're okay? Do you need anything?" The softness in her voice threw Ash for a minute.

Jessica Kirk had always been the strong one, in charge of the three sisters from the time they were little. She was the director of all their backyard plays, the ruler of the tree fort and the sandbox. She was the one who tattled to Mom and Dad, the one who doled out cookies after dinner, the one who turned off the porch light if her younger sisters stayed out after dark. She'd been six going on sixteen going on forty, even back then.

"I'm okay, thanks. But I have to go. Tell Anne I said hi."

"Tell her yourself," Jess said. "You don't have to ignore her too."

Ash hung up before she could work up to words she knew she'd regret. She grabbed the groceries and hauled them to her apartment. She dropped everything on the kitchen counter and headed for the shower, pulling off her clothes as she went. She could picture Jess dialing their other sister, gossiping about where poor little Ash had ended up. They'd laugh, the two of them, with their wonderful law degrees and gung-ho political campaigns. They'd laugh and wonder how Ash had turned out so different from the rest of the Kirk family.

She turned on the shower, left it cold, and stepped under the stream of water. The chill took her breath away, and for an instant she was glad. At least goose bumps might make her forget where she was. Eddie. The blonde. Her father. Jess. Ash let the water run down her back and shivered. At that particular moment, everything in her life seemed twisted up and wrong.

Every single thing.

Chapter Ten

Ash turned the key in the ignition. Nothing. Not a single sound. Not a click or a cough. "Damn!"

Forty minutes past midnight, and here she sat in the back parking lot of Blues and Booze with a car that wouldn't start. She supposed she'd pushed her luck, what with the sluggish way it had turned over the last few days. Frustrated, she slapped one hand against the steering wheel. No hope now. The thing was completely dead. She glanced at the moon, nearly full. She supposed she could walk home. Everyone kept telling her how safe Paradise was after dark. It was only three blocks back to Lycian Street, anyway.

She climbed out again, made sure the windows were rolled up and locked her doors. Thunder had rumbled over Paradise for most of the night, and the last thing she needed was her leather interior ruined by rain. Glancing at her watch, she started across the parking lot.

She'd taken only a few steps when she saw him in the shadows, a man with his hands stuffed in his pockets, watching her. Ash froze. Her stomach clenched with panic, and a thin layer of perspiration broke out on her upper lip. Paradise safe after dark? Yeah, right. Her first night walking home, and she was about to be mugged. Close to eighty dollars in singles bulged in her right front pocket, gas and grocery money for the following week. If this guy stole it, she'd have six dollars to her name. Ash took a step back.

She'd taken a self-defense course back in college; what had the instructor always said?

Do not act or look like an easy target...be confident.

She lifted her chin, eyes darting from side to side.

Do not let yourself get blocked in...always have an escape route.

Ash considered her choices. She could cross the lot and follow Main Street down to the square, cutting behind the church and winding home the back way. She could make her way to Palmetto, the street running behind her, and head for the train station. Sometimes a cab idled there as it waited for late arrivals. Or she could get back in her car, lock all the doors, and call the police from her cell phone.

Forget that last one. She didn't need to attract any attention from local authorities. They'd take one look at her driver's license and identify her as Senator Kirk's daughter right away. By the following morning, everyone in town would know who she was. And the jokes would start all over again.

As she stood in the shadowy lot, heart pummeling against her breastbone, the man began to move toward her. Thick arms hung from a solid frame, and he walked with purpose. Oh, God. Forget about the money. What if he grabbed her? What if he tried to rape her?

She wrapped her right hand around her car keys, working the sharp edges so that they pointed straight at him. Maybe she could stab him between the eyes. Maybe she could kick him in the groin and then stab him between the eyes. Maybe she could—

"Ash? What are you doing back here?"

Her heart leapt at his words, an instant before it puddled around her ankles. "Eddie! You scared the hell out of me." She'd never been so happy to see anyone in her life. Suddenly boneless, her hand flapped against her leg. Her keys slipped through shaking fingers and fell to the ground.

He bent down and scooped them up. "It's way past twelve."

"I know." She waved in the direction of her lifeless car. "It wouldn't start."

He frowned. "You should have told me."

The concern in his voice washed over her, smooth and warm. The tightness that had rolled around in her stomach the last few days vanished.

"I didn't want to bother you." She paused. "What are you doing here, anyway?"

Eddie dropped his chin, suddenly fascinated with his shoelaces. He put a hand on the back of his neck, opened his mouth, and then closed it again without saying anything. When he answered after a long minute, his voice was gruff. "Knew you weren't home. Wanted to make sure you were okay."

Ash bit her bottom lip as her cheeks flamed. He'd been sitting up? Waiting for her? Worrying about her? She smiled. "Yeah, I'm okay. Just tired."

"So let's go." Dropping one arm across her shoulders, he pulled her close, squeezing for a moment before backing away again. "I'll come down, take a look at your car tomorrow morning."

"Really? Thanks."

They headed across the lot to where it opened onto Main Street and walked in silence. Ash tried to keep her short stride up with Eddie's longer one. Curiosity got the better of her after a few minutes. "What happened to Savannah?"

He didn't answer.

"Eddie? Hello?" Maybe she'd gotten the name wrong.

"It was just a date," he said.

"Oh." Ash dodged a trashcan that had rolled into the sidewalk. "You gonna see her again?"

He glanced over. "Don't know. Maybe."

"That's a no." She elbowed him. "What's wrong with you?"

He stopped short on the corner of Elm Street. "Nothing, last time I checked. Why?"

"You know you're totally self-destructive, right?"

"What're you talking about?"

"This whole thing where you go out with women once or twice, show them a good time, get them thinking maybe you like them, and then never go out with them again…"

"I like women, Ash. What's wrong with that? One date doesn't mean I want to get serious with anyone. I like to keep my options open."

"Well, that's obvious."

He frowned. "Now you're mad at me? Are we fighting again?"

"No. Sorry. I just meant…you give women the wrong idea, I think."

"I never make promises. Not to any of them."

Yeah, I know. That's what breaks their hearts.

A white pick-up truck missing a taillight rolled past them. The horn beeped, and Eddie raised a hand in greeting.

"You know him?"

He laughed. "Know just about everyone in Paradise."

Ash considered that for a minute. "Does it ever bother you? You ever want to live somewhere else? Somewhere people don't know your business?" The question, from deep in her soul, burned as it crossed her lips.

He shrugged. "Not really. Thought about it a couple of times, but I'm settled here, you know?"

They walked a few more paces.

"Thing is," Eddie continued, "I don't think other places, small towns or big cities, are any better at hiding out in."

She jerked at his words and stumbled over a tree root growing through the pavement. "I didn't say anything about hiding out."

"No, I know." He waved a hand. "I just meant that…well…everyone thinks the grass is greener. If they live in a small town, they think they got to move to a city. If they live in a city, they think a place like Paradise is better. Less scandal or corruption or something. But I gotta tell you, people have the same problems no matter where they go. Big city or small town, people get hurt. Friends steal from each other. Men cheat on their wives. Kids sneak out at night and get drunk while their parents think they're sleeping. People get divorced, leave home, desert their kids. And people sure as hell die, same as every other place."

He looked at the sky, as if counting the stars strewn out like a map above them. "At least here in Paradise, you know someone's got your back. You know there's always someone you can count on, someone you grew up with who's gonna forgive you no matter how bad you screw things up." They turned the corner onto Lycian Street. "So no, I've never really wanted to live anywhere else."

Ash thought about that as they turned into the walk leading up to their house. Safety in a small town, huh? She wasn't sure she could believe it. But then again, why had she moved here, and why was she staying, unless something about the way a no-name village drew its arms around her felt right? She glanced sideways at her neighbor. For a guy who hadn't ever left his hometown, Eddie West sure seemed to know a lot about the ways in which the world worked.

"Thanks for walking me home."

"No problem." He dug his hands into his pockets. One dimple popped as he smiled at her.

"See you tomorrow, I guess."

"See ya."

She felt his eyes on her back all the way up the stairs.

* * *

Eddie pulled into the employee parking lot behind Frank's Imports just shy of nine the next morning. Ash's car, he saw, had been towed and dropped in front of the shop. *Good.* He pulled on a faded blue baseball cap and headed inside.

"What's up with the Volkswagen?" Frank sat behind his desk, feet propped up, hands laced behind his bald head, an unlit cigar clamped between his teeth.

"Belongs to a friend of mine."

"You better take care of Mrs. Myer's oil leak first."

"I got it. Don't worry."

Ash showed up an hour later, cheeks flushed and her hair pulled into a ponytail. Running shorts brushed the tops of toned legs, and a tank top curved around damp breasts. From the other side of the shop, Eddie swallowed and told himself to think of cold showers.

"West!" Frank hollered.

"Hang on."

"You got a visitor!" Frank crossed the room and kicked at his foot. Eddie wheeled the creeper out from under the sedan he was working on. "You didn't tell me your friend was a chick," his boss said, in a voice that echoed in the cavernous space. "A cute one."

Eddie cut a glance Ash's way and watched her smile. "Yeah? There's a reason for that."

"Hi," Ash said when he approached. "I was out for a run, thought I'd stop by and see what I owed you."

Eddie pulled a rag from his back pocket, aware of the dirt on his hands and the smell of gasoline on his clothes. She looked fresh, alive, young around the eyes in a way that she hadn't when they'd first moved in. He liked it.

"Haven't had a chance to look at it yet. Sorry."

"Oh." She raised her arms, stretching over her head. "That's okay. I can come back." Her shirt pulled up a little, and for a moment all Eddie wanted to do was run a hand across that strip of skin above her waistband.

With effort, he pulled his gaze away and checked the clock. "Maybe around lunchtime? Can you come back after one?"

"Sure." She looked around, taking in the enormous steel toolboxes, the hoses hanging from the wall, and the lifts with cars sitting on them in various states of repair. Eddie watched her catalog it all and wondered what she thought.

"Do you—would you like me to bring lunch? I sort of feel like I owe you." Ash wiped her forehead with the back of one wrist.

"I haven't fixed anything yet."

She cocked her head. "Yeah, but you had it towed here. And you saved me last night."

"What, from all the muggers in Paradise?"

She smiled, and Eddie loved the way it lit up her face, turning her eyes from brown to green. Desire kneed him right in the gut. "Exactly. So do you want pizza or subs?"

He shrugged. He didn't much care, if it meant he was going to see her again soon. "You decide."

She turned to leave. "Okay, but remember you said that."

He watched the sway in her step until she disappeared. Then he eased himself back under Mrs. Myers' car. Oil leaks. That's what he needed to be thinking about. Not good-looking upstairs neighbors. Not long legs and eyes so big he could lose himself inside them. And definitely not small waists or smiles that ended with a biting of the bottom lip and pink that spread from cheek to cheek when she laughed.

Eddie reached for a wrench and adjusted his droplight, trying to ignore the throbbing in his groin. When he scraped open a knuckle a few minutes later, he was glad for the pain that drove Ash from his thoughts once and for all.

Chapter Eleven

"I got both," Ash said two hours later, her arms filled with bags from Lou's Sub Shop and a six-pack of soda. Behind her, on Frank's desk, Eddie spied the corner of a pizza box. His stomach rumbled, but not before the scent of her, feminine and floral, drifted over to him.

"Great. Smells terrific."

He headed for the sink in the corner and spent a few extra minutes scrubbing. *Jesus, why does she do that to me?* He glanced at his reflection in the paper towel dispenser. Why did Ash leave him stuttering around like a fool? Women never threw Eddie West into a tailspin. Usually it was the other way around. Usually they fell for him, called him, waited around for him. But ever since Ash had moved in upstairs, things had changed. He felt unsteady on his feet around her. And the trouble was, they weren't even dating. A heavy whisper of possibility just hung over every moment they spent together. Eddie splashed water on his face. Did she feel it too?

"You don't get your ass over here, I'm gonna eat the whole pie and both subs," Frank called across the shop.

"Like hell you will." Eddie pulled up a chair and propped one knee against the desk. Ash sat a few feet away, a salad balanced on her lap. She'd changed into one of those halter-tops that clung to her curves, one that made him see swells in all the right places. A pair of shorts, frayed around the hem, rode up on her thighs. Eddie reached for a soda and forced himself to look away.

"It's the distributor cap," he said after a few mouthfuls of Italian sub.

"On my car?" Ash said. "Is that bad?"

He shook his head. "Nope. Take me ten minutes to replace it."

"That's it?"

He finished the sub and reached for a slice of pizza. "That's it."

"How much will it cost?"

He thought about teasing her, about telling her she couldn't afford it unless she meant to spend the next week cooking him dinner. But he couldn't. The way she looked at him, with that wide, trusting expression, twisted his heart halfway around. "Forty bucks."

Frank snorted. "For the part, maybe." He winked at Ash. "Guess he's throwing in the labor for free. Must be your lucky day." The telephone rang, and he reached over to answer it.

Eddie watched the blush spread its way across Ash's cheeks, enjoying the way it made her eyes shine.

"Thanks," she said to Eddie, as Frank stood to take the call on the other side of the office. "I really appreciate it. You have no idea."

"Better than having it towed back to your mechanic in Boston."

The way she started in her chair caught him off guard.

"What do—oh." She raised a hand to smooth a few curls away from her face. "Right."

"You have someone you take it to, regular?" Eddie asked. *There's that look again. Like she has to watch her words. Or watch her back.* Ash hadn't told him anything about her life before Paradise. In fact, she avoided it every time he brought it up. But her silence, and those nervous glances every now and again, made him more curious than if she'd dropped hints and tried to tease him into guessing the details of her story. And everyone had a story. He knew that better than anyone.

She shrugged. "I usually just take it to whoever I can find."

Frank hung up the phone and scrawled something on the giant calendar that hung on the office wall. "Everyone's god-damned air conditioning goes at the same time," he grumbled. "God forbid anyone thinks about trying it out before June. Then they get their panties in a knot 'cause I can't see 'em until next week. What the hell do they expect?"

Ash laughed.

"So how you liking Paradise?" Eddie's boss returned to his chair, springs creaking under his giant frame, and laced thick fingers behind his head as he leaned backwards.

"It's nice."

Frank grimaced. "Don't know how nice it is if you're used to livin' in a city. 'Less you been born here, I can't see there's much reason to stick around."

"No, really, I like it," Ash insisted. She turned to look out the plate glass window behind them. "The square, and all the little shops downtown, and…" Her voice drifted off, and suddenly, Eddie felt sorry for her.

"Guess every place has some redeeming qualities, huh?" he finished for her.

She glanced up at him. "Guess so."

"Hey, how's this for a crazy idea?" he said after a minute.

"What?"

"Let's have a party."

A furrow appeared between her eyes. "What kind?"

"A regular party. At our place. With lots of food and lots of beer and—" He pulled off his baseball cap and rubbed his head. "It'll be like a housewarming party. We can have it outside, on the porch roof."

She thought a minute. "Actually, that's not a bad idea. Jen told me it was the perfect place. I think it needs some work, though. There's loose boards in that one corner, and the big patch with no paint..."

He shrugged. "No biggie. We can do some repairs."

"Jen's brother Lucas is really good at all that. I could ask him if he could come up for a day. I mean, so you don't have to worry about it."

"Either way's fine." He grinned, loving the idea already. "So it's settled."

"Do it for Fourth of July," Frank suggested.

Ash cocked her head. "I like it." Her gaze met Eddie's and washed over him.

He cleared his throat, and though he wanted to say something else, wanted to keep the connection hovering between them, he didn't have a chance. The bell on the front door rang, and Cassandra Perkins breezed in, with a sweep of auburn hair and a perky little ass sashaying below it. Eddie cringed.

Cass. Great. The last person he needed to see. Too much history there. He wished suddenly he could rewind the day, just five minutes in reverse, so he could lock the door and keep that part of his past where it belonged. Then he could watch Ash laugh, watch the way she tucked her hair behind her ears, and spend the rest of the afternoon remembering her smile and thinking about the way it burned him clear through to the core.

* * *

The buxom redhead wiggled her way across the office, leaving a cloud of cloying perfume in her wake. Ash inched back in her chair, to give the scent and the woman attached to it some room.

"Hi, darlin'." She bent over and planted a kiss in the center of Eddie's forehead. Pendulous breasts swayed from a tube top that had inched its way down from almost-modest to porn star wannabe.

Eddie turned almost purple with discomfort. "Hi yourself, Cassandra. What the hell are you doing here?"

The redhead tossed her hair. One hand tugged at her top. The other dropped to her hip and hung there. "Stopping by to say hi, that's all." She pushed out her lips in a faux pout. "It's been a while. You haven't stopped by the salon."

Eddie shrugged. "Don't need a haircut."

Cassandra plopped herself onto his lap. She twined one arm around his neck and began running her fingers through the waves that fell around his ears. "Oh, I might argue with that," she purred. One leg crossed over the other, and she gave a throaty laugh. "Been longer than six weeks, hasn't it?"

Eddie placed two large hands on her hips and steered her back to a stand. "Lunch break's over. I gotta work."

Undeterred, the twenty-something siren twisted a lock of hair around an artificial fingernail, painted bright pink. "I'm still waiting on that rain check you promised me."

Ash's chest tightened. She tried to look away and couldn't. For a few moments during lunch, she'd almost felt as though she belonged here, in Eddie's world. Talking to him, laughing with Frank, watching the same mothers roll the same strollers back and forth down the sidewalk, she'd almost felt a niche begin to carve itself out. In the last few weeks, she'd begun to know her way around Paradise. She'd begun to understand the flavor of the people who lived here. And part of her—a big part of her—had begun to like it.

But one look at this woman reminded her how far she was from home.

"Aw, get off him, Cass," Frank said. "Can't you see he's got a friend here?"

For the first time, the woman turned toward Ash. A long look up and down, through heavy-lidded eyes drenched with mascara, and her smile disappeared. Without saying a word, she tossed her hair again. This time, though, the motion held less flirtation and more simmering jealousy.

"So? I can't stop by and say hello to my boyfriend during his lunch break?"

Eddie stuffed his baseball cap back onto his head as he stood. "I'm not your boyfriend, Cass."

Sidling up to him, she wound one arm through his and leveled an unmistakable look at Ash. "Maybe not at the moment, sweetheart. But even the best lovers need some time apart, hmm?" Her chin lifted, and she stood on tiptoes until her lips brushed his cheek. Her next words were a stage whisper, loud enough for everyone in the room to hear.

"Don't forget who was there for you that night. Don't forget who held your hand when the doctors told you there was nothing else they could do. And don't forget what you told me the morning after. Take as much time as you need. When you're ready, I'll be here."

Chapter Twelve

Eddie felt her gaze on him before he awoke, beyond the twitching and the feeling of falling that always plagued him in these dreams. Nightmares, he corrected himself in the fog of sleepiness. Not dreams. No dreams could haunt him, day after day, night after night, the way these did. Behind his eyelids they played: one red light, like the eye of an indifferent god, changing to green—he was sure it was green—and then glass shattering and the wail of a siren. Finally, his brother's moans.

Eddie lunged up from the loveseat, eyes wide open, fingers damp with perspiration punching into empty air. Ash sat next to him and stared.

"Eddie?" Her voice was quiet, fearful.

He sank into the cushions, took a deep breath, and tried to push the nightmare away.

"What was that?" Her eyes grew larger as he fought to breathe normally.

"Ah, just a bad dream." He tried to laugh it off.

"In the middle of the day?"

He loosened his fingers from the fists they'd tightened themselves into. "Sometimes." Maybe someday he'd tell her about the horror that had haunted him the past three years. Maybe. Right now it was still too painful to revisit.

"Sorry I dozed off." He glanced at the television. Bottom of the eighth inning. How long had he been sleeping? Twenty minutes? Longer? Since the Sox were up in the sixth.

"Don't be," Ash answered. "You've been working twelve-hour days all week."

Eddie rolled his head, neck stiff. "No kidding." He checked his watch. Almost four. "You working tonight?"

"Yeah. Told Marty I'd come in around five-thirty. He hired another new girl, asked me to train her." She paused. "Can I ask you something?"

Eddie winced. He hoped whatever question Ash had worked up during his nap wasn't too probing or painful. Just thinking about opening the memory of Cal again, a rusty tin can with sharp, bloody edges, stole his breath. That's what he got for falling asleep. She'd figure out what had happened sooner or later. If he didn't tell her himself, she'd guess from the nightmares.

But to his relief, Ash's question didn't have anything to do with that. "What's the story with that woman from the shop?"

Eddie's cheeks heated up. "Cassandra?"

"The redhead who stopped in the other day, yeah."

He cocked his head, not wanting to answer right away. "Why? You jealous?"

"Please." She narrowed her eyes. "So what's the deal?"

"We dated a while back."

"So I gathered."

"And then we broke up."

"Does she know that?"

"She should. She's the reason it happened."

* * *

Eddie had let himself in the back door of her apartment, the same way he always had when he stopped by after work. This time, though, Cass wasn't waiting for him. She wasn't standing in the kitchen, frying pork chops in her black bra and his red plaid boxer shorts. She wasn't sitting in the living room, a glass of wine in one hand for her and a cold beer in the other for him. A strange stillness filled the apartment for a fraction of a second. Then he noticed the sounds.

They came from the bedroom, low laughter and the swish of fabric on fabric. Eddie looked at the clock above the sink, the dishtowels below it, the cutting board, unwashed, lying on the counter. The laughter changed to soft moans, and a humming grew in his ears. He flipped on the hall switch, and too-bright light chased shadows from the pictures Cass had hung on the walls from last summer's vacation. He'd walked down the hall and stopped in the open bedroom doorway. A man he didn't know lay in bed on top of his girlfriend. Cass took one look at Eddie and yanked up the sheet.

She'd yelled at him as if it were his fault he'd walked in on them. He wondered how long it had been going on, and how stupid and blind he'd been not to see it sooner. She'd tried calling him at work and later at his parents', but he wouldn't talk to her. He returned to the apartment only once, to get a few lousy things he thought probably belonged to him, and that was it.

He hoped he never saw the bitch again.

* * *

Ash raised her eyebrows as Eddie finished the story. "Rough. Sorry."

"Me too. Doesn't matter."

"You sure about that? Looks like she's interested in a second chance."

He shifted on the couch. One bare ankle brushed Ash's, and he drew it back before his mind went in directions it shouldn't. "Damn sure. Cass might want to get back together, but I'm done with her."

Don't forget who was there for you that night. Don't forget who held your hand when the doctors told you there was nothing else they could do.

Eddie hoped Ash wasn't thinking of what Cass had said the other day. He couldn't explain. He couldn't tell her, that yeah, Cass had come to the hospital the night of the accident. She'd waited for him to wake up, and then she'd held his hand when the doctor came in and told them about his brother. She'd wiped away his tears when he couldn't find the strength to do it himself. She'd let him sleep at her place for days at a time, pulling the blankets over him when he kicked them off in nightmares so violent he'd wake up shivering. But so what? She'd cheated on him, too, less than six months later, so what did that say about her devotion?

Ash was asking him something. Eddie fought back the fog of anger and tried to focus. "Sorry. What?"

"I just wondered if you've ever had a serious girlfriend. In your life?"

"Depends on how you define serious. "Not really. Cass was close for a while, but..." He didn't know how to finish. What good did it do to get attached to someone, if you knew that someday they'd betray you, turn their back and leave? Everyone left at some point. Girlfriends. Family. Even the people you thought you could count on forever, like brothers. Especially brothers.

"What about you?" he asked, filling the silence.

She dropped her gaze, same as always. Ash never wanted to talk about herself. She just wanted to finesse other people into telling all their secrets. Just like a lawyer.

"Serious boyfriend? This one you just broke up with?"

She shrugged. "I thought so." She picked at a hole in the arm of the loveseat. "Guess I was wrong." Sadness filled the spaces in her face that before had held light.

"His loss," Eddie said.

"That's what I keep trying to tell myself."

"You decide how long you're staying in town?" He tried to convince himself it was a casual question, that it didn't matter to him one way or the other who lived upstairs from him. Truth was, though, Eddie couldn't imagine anyone but Ash tripping down those stairs in the morning, letting herself in after dark, tossing a toy for the kitten to play with. He couldn't picture anyone else on the other side of this door, anyone else stretching out on the rooftop, anyone else arguing about whose turn it was to drag the trashcan to the corner.

She'd gotten under his skin.

"I don't know," she said after a minute. "I only sublet through the summer, so when September rolls around…"

She didn't finish, and Eddie wasn't sure he wanted her to.

"Well, you'll figure it out," he said and left it at that.

She laid her head against the cushions and closed her eyes. "I hope so," she said, but the words were so quiet he wondered if she'd meant to speak them aloud at all.

Chapter Thirteen

"Marty had to go outta town," J.T. informed Ash as soon as she walked into the restaurant that evening.

"Oh. Okay." She wasn't sure what that had to do with her.

"He said you're supposed to be in charge 'til he gets back." J.T. stuck a toothpick into his mouth and wiped down the empty bar.

Ash stopped. "What are you talking about?"

The bartender flipped a glass and slid it into place on the shelf. "Here." He fished in his front pocket for a slip of paper. Ash recognized Marty's scrawl on the back of the wrinkled receipt as J.T. handed it over.

Ash, please take over tonight. You know where the keys are. Money goes in the safe. Be back tomorrow. M.

She sagged onto a stool. "Why me?"

The bartender shrugged. "Why not?"

Ash dropped her head onto one hand and stared at the note. *Take over?* Well, how hard could it be, really, to empty out the two registers at the end of the night and lock up the money? She knew the rest of the routine: how to wipe down and secure everything in the kitchen, where to put the trash out back, how to set the alarm when she left. Marty had shown her all that weeks ago. Bobby V., the kitchen's head cook, had worked at the place longer than Marty had run it. And J.T. was in charge of the bar.

"Okay." She headed for the kitchen. She'd give it a try. Tuesdays never drew a big crowd anyway. And it didn't look as though she had much choice. How much could she screw up in a single night? "You all set out here?"

J.T. winked when she glanced back at him. "All set, boss."

She gave him a dirty look and decided not to answer.

* * *

"You did good," the bartender said a few hours later. They sat across from each other and stared at an infomercial scrolling across the television screen.

"Yeah? Thanks." Exhausted but secretly pleased with herself, Ash reviewed the night. Only a handful of tables, but that wasn't unusual for a weekday, and J.T. had done a decent business at the bar. She'd even managed to handle Betty June, the widow who complained about everything from the temperature of her steak to the number of ice cubes in her drink. By the end of her meal, thanks to a couple of questions about her cats and a compliment of her wide-brimmed hat, the woman had practically beamed at Ash as she left.

"You should be in charge more often." J.T. stacked glasses. "You're damn better lookin' than Marty, anyway."

"Maybe he'll give me a raise."

The bartender laughed. "Keep dreaming, honey."

Ash laughed too. "I guess you're right." Still, she wouldn't mind the extra responsibility. It had been nice, moving about the dining room, checking on customers, answering the phone, and organizing the kitchen in a way she didn't dare when the manager hung over her shoulder. It made her feel like she wasn't completely wasting her summer.

Part-time night manager at Blues and Booze? Not a bad way to spend the next few weeks. Maybe she'd talk to Marty about it after all.

* * *

The following night, Ash lay in the bathtub and ran a washcloth across her stomach. Bare toenails peeked at her from beneath the bubbles. She balanced her head on the edge of the tub and let her hair float on the water around her chin. Closing her eyes, she breathed in the waves of raspberry from the candles that flickered on the windowsill. Etta James sang to her from the living room. She hummed to the music and let herself float until the water began to cool.

She hadn't seen Eddie at all today, but she guessed he'd probably agreed to a double shift at the shop, since he was taking tomorrow off for their party. She couldn't wait to tell him about the manager position. She'd asked Marty about it earlier, and he'd nearly fallen over in agreement. The stingy guy had even agreed to pay her fifty cents more an hour. Ash smiled and wondered what her sisters, with their six-figure salaries, would say if they knew. She sank lower in the tub and decided she didn't care. For the first time in her life, she'd chosen her own path, one that curved away from the Kirk family one. So what if it only lasted for a month or so? She still liked the way it felt.

The ring of her cell phone woke her. One wet hand emerged from the water and lifted it from the bathmat. Jen, probably. Ash didn't bother to look at the screen. *She's probably checking to see what time she and Lucas should get here tomorrow.* Or maybe it was Eddie, remembering one more thing he wanted to bring for food. Ash smiled.

"Hello?"

For a moment she heard nothing but silence on the other end of the line. Then a too-familiar voice spoke her name. Her real name. "Ashton?"

Colin. Oh my God. Her eyes flew open, and she sat up in the tub, shaking. Ash stared at the phone as if it had suddenly grown a mouth all its own. For a moment, she thought about hanging up. She didn't owe Colin anything. He hadn't called her in almost two months. She didn't want to give him the satisfaction of hearing her voice.

But she couldn't hang up. Instead she sat there, dripping, hand frozen to the phone.

"Ash, it's me."

As if she didn't know. As if she could forget the voice that had broken her heart just a few months earlier.

"I know who it is." She pulled the plug from the drain and reached for a towel, shivering as cool air brushed her damp skin.

"How've you been?" He sounded nervous, and she was glad.

What's with the small talk? "I'm fine."

"That's good." He cleared his throat. "How are your sisters?"

You should know, considering you talked to Jess a couple of weeks ago. "They're fine too, I guess." She paused. "What do you want?"

"I..." Colin hesitated. "I miss you."

Ash dropped the towel and headed into her bedroom. *Like hell you do.* He wanted something. Or he needed something. He couldn't have gotten tired of Callie already. She stuck her arms through the sleeves of her robe and sank onto the bed. Rubbing her temple with one hand, she tried to squelch the other thought that insisted on rearing its head.

I miss you too.

"What am I supposed to say to that? You made it pretty clear two months ago that you wanted time. Space. Callie Halliway." She spoke the name without breaking and was proud of herself. "Besides, you were so embarrassed by everything that happened with my father that you couldn't wait to get away from it all. Remember?"

"I made a mistake. Please. It's over with me and Callie. It never was much of anything to begin with."

"That's supposed to make me feel better?"

"Jess told me you took a summer place somewhere up north. Tell me where it is. I'll come up. Tomorrow. Tonight. Or you come home. Please." His words spilled out, anxious and awkward. "I want us to try again. I was wrong...I'm sorry."

Ash closed her eyes. *Don't say that.* She couldn't bear to hear the remorse in Colin's voice. She couldn't afford to give in to his pleas, not after working so hard to get over him. And yet she couldn't resist them either, despite her best efforts. Sighing, she let the weight of memory roll across her heart. In a flash, it all came back: Colin's serious expression above her in bed, his hands in her hair, his cheek twitching at the beginning of a smile. His arm around her waist as they crossed campus. His wink as they took notes through class, side by side. His name. His family. God, she'd fallen so hard, so fast, without a thought of what might come after the breathlessness.

After the letter, she'd begun the grim task of shuttering up her heart, piling brick upon brick to seal out the hurt. Now here he was, calling and pretending an apology and a little attention could make everything all right? Brittle tears made their way up her throat.

"Ashton?"

"I can't do this."

"Please—"

"I'm not telling you where I am. And I'm not coming home. I need to figure things out." She picked at a thread in her quilt.

"I miss you," he said again, and the words tore at her heart.

She pictured Colin's eyes, liquid and pleading. Her resolve weakened. Maybe it wasn't too late. Maybe she should give him a second chance.

"Will you at least think about it?"

She took a deep breath. *No,* she wanted to say. *I won't think about it. It's over, and I'm moving on without you.* But the pull of his voice and the memories it held were too strong.

"Maybe." The thread yanked free from the quilt and left a tiny hole in the pink fabric. She twisted it around her finger and wondered how much of a mistake she was making. "Maybe I'll think about it."

"I really want to work things out."

She tightened her hand around the phone. "I have to go." She hung up before he could say anything else.

Stunned, unable to form any kind of coherent thought, Ash pulled down the window shade and sat in silence. *Colin...after all this time.* She rolled onto her stomach and pressed her face into the pillow. Tears welled up, and this time, she let them come. Maybe on another day, she would have known better, would have turned up the music on the stereo, would have opened all the windows to let evening light flood in. Maybe on another day, she would have turned her back on that piece of her life that still bled when she poked at the scar.

But it wasn't another day. It wasn't far enough from the past. Ash was a Kirk daughter, a Harvard graduate, and she'd had every intention of marrying Colin Parker. She'd planned on opening a joint law practice with him, having his children, moving into his family's estate with the wide porch and thriving flowerbeds. Until two months ago.

He wants me back? He wants to try again?

A few weeks ago, Ash would have leapt into his arms. But now? Now, she didn't know. To her surprise, a few weeks in Paradise had started to change things. She stared into the blackness behind her eyelids and pursed her lips until Colin's face disappeared, and she could no longer hear his voice ringing against the hollow behind her cheekbones. She took a deep breath and opened her eyes. For the moment, he was gone. Now she just had to figure out how to make him stay there.

Chapter Fourteen

"Lucas, it's perfect." Ash wrapped her arms around Jen's younger brother. "Thank you so, so much for coming up and helping out."

"Aw, didn't do much," he said gruffly. The six-foot-seven giant turned three shades of red as Ash released him.

"Yeah, you did." The porch still smelled of fresh paint, and all the loose boards had been fixed, along with the leaking toilet and the stuck window in Ash's bedroom, which he definitely hadn't had to do.

Lucas ran one hand over a head full of curly dark hair. "It's a nice apartment." He leaned against the railing and stared at the street. Always solemn, he seemed quieter than ever today. Broken hearts tended to do that, Ash supposed.

"Yeah," she agreed. "Hey, you're gonna stay for the party, right?" She was almost positive Eddie had some single friends she could steer in Lucas's direction.

"Naw, I gotta get back." He pulled a baseball cap from his back pocket and stuck it on lopsidedly. "Mom an' Dad are havin' a barbeque later. Told 'em I'd try to make it." He grinned. "It's always hit and miss with Dad and the grill. I'd rather see him keep his eyebrows tonight."

She laughed. Such a good guy. She still couldn't believe his girlfriend had cheated on him. In another life, Ash might have considered letting Jen set her up with Lucas, the way she'd been trying to since about the second week the two of them had lived together. Ridiculously tall, seriously built, and sweet down to the core – what woman in her right mind would cheat on someone like that?

Ash straightened the tables in both corners of the porch roof as Lucas planted a kiss goodbye on the top of her head. Guess you never really knew the thoughts in people's heads. Secrets hid, lies grew, and sometimes the very people you thought you knew best were the ones burying their knives in your back. *Or their hearts in someone else's.*

She shook away the thought. Not tonight. No sadness, and no regret. She glanced into the street below. A few cars already lined the curb in front of the house, and the sun hadn't even begun to set. Apparently, thanks to Eddie, half of Paradise had been invited to their housewarming party.

A few minutes later, he poked his head through the window, looking out from the kitchen. "Ash? Everything good out here?"

"I think so." She and Jen had spent most of the afternoon decorating. Now red, white, and blue lights twisted themselves around the porch railing. Flags perched in buckets of ice, while picnic benches and tables bowed under piles of food and soft drinks.

"Jen's brother's not staying?"

She shook her head.

Eddie rested both arms on the sill. "Seems like a nice guy."

"He is."

"You and he ever…" He didn't finish the question, but she read the look on his face.

"Me and Lucas? God, no. He's like – I mean, he's Jen's little brother."

"So?"

"So nothing." She propped one hand on a hip. "Are you jealous?"

"Nope. Just curious."

She grabbed a handful of ice from the nearest cooler and tossed it in his direction. "Whatever."

"I'm gonna run out and get the beer," he said. He picked up a few slivers of ice, already melting, and palmed them. "Like it wet, huh?"

Ash turned away before the blush spread across her face. "You wish." She wrestled with the cooler, trying to drag it to the other end of the porch, and ended up dumping half the ice onto her feet.

Behind her, Eddie laughed as he retreated from the window. "As I was saying."

"Shut up," she said, but she started to laugh herself.

Jen looked over from the far corner of the porch, where she was arranging napkins and silverware. "So when are the two of you going to stop playing this game?"

Ash gave up on the cooler and left it where it was. "What game?"

"Please. That guy has been up here five times today. He's called you twice. Why don't you just sleep with him and get it over with?" Jen dropped the last stack of napkins into place.

"God, Jen, everything does not always have to be about sex."

Jen smirked. "Okay, fine. Don't sleep with him. But why don't you at least go out with him? See a movie or something. Spend a little time playing doctor after work. He's seriously gorgeous. And single, right? What the hell are you waiting for?"

Ash tried not to smile, tried not to reveal that she'd let some of the same thoughts drift across her mind the last few weeks. "It's not like that with me and Eddie. We're just friends. Housemates. He's not really my type, anyway," she lied.

"Right." Jen's voice dripped with sarcasm. "Good looking, good job, monster biceps, funny—not your type at all."

"Anyway, I think he's involved with someone," Ash added.

"Who?"

"I don't know. But he's always got a girl down there." *Except when he's up here with me, watching a ball game or having a beer or...*Ash shook her head. Eddie West was Paradise's playboy. Didn't matter that he happened to be her housemate as well. He loved women, in any variety and any package, and the more the better, from what she'd observed. Just about everyone in town seemed to know it, and she'd be better off remembering that.

"Come on," she said, ignoring Jen's gaze. "Let's start making the appetizers."

* * *

By nine o'clock, nearly everyone had arrived, and most of the guests had moved out onto the roof. The party was in full swing, with classic rock pouring out of the speakers and laughter carrying up to the treetops. Ash looked around at the smiling faces: some regulars from the restaurant, a few of Eddie's high school friends, and a couple of neighbors from around the corner.

Someone bumped her from behind, a burly man with a huge red beard. "Oops! Sorry, sweetheart. Great party, by the way."

"Thanks." Ash smiled at the crowd, so different from the people she'd grown up with, the snobby elite who threw cocktail parties and talked politics inside their gated communities. The conversations around her buzzed with baseball predictions and comments on the weather, news about the latest divorce and the shopping center scheduled to break ground next month. People cursed and laughed and wound their arms around each other; they tossed back shots of tequila and played cards in the corner.

It startled Ash to realize how comfortable she felt here after only a few weeks. How real people seemed when you peeled away layers of presumption, when you paid attention to each other for the things you cared about and not the things you had.

She pushed her way through the bodies clustered around the stereo and found a space near the porch railing. She knew only a fraction of the guests by name, but she didn't really mind. She'd catch up with Eddie in a minute or two, see if they needed to make another run to the store for anything. But at the moment, she wanted a few minutes to breathe. July had snuck up on her when she wasn't looking, and she knew that after the fireworks vanished, August would steal along in its place. Then September would round the corner, hand-in-hand with a life she wasn't sure she wanted to meet.

"Ashton, please call home," her mother had said on her voicemail last night. "We haven't heard from you in weeks. Is everything okay? Please..."

She'd erased the message before her mother finished talking. What was she supposed to say? How could she begin to explain her decision? Funny how it became easier every day to pretend she belonged in Paradise, to pretend she came from a normal family and had no secrets to hide.

Ash turned up the stereo volume another notch and dug a cold beer from the bottom of the cooler. She stared across the street to the shadowed park that backed up to Helen's house. It was quiet for a Saturday. Usually she and Eddie spied a few kids there on the weekends, sneaking joints, making out, talking loudly in that adolescent voice that cracked and wavered and flirted and bullied. She laughed at them, wondered about them. Sometimes she even envied them a little.

Everything is so exciting when you're sixteen, so fresh and painful. Your skin aches with wanting, and every sunrise, every phone call, every heartbreak, cuts you a little deeper. As a grown-up, she'd almost forgotten how a mere breath of wind at the right moment could bring tears to her eyes.

Tonight, though, the swings hung unnaturally still, and only a stray cat wound its way through the legs of a picnic table before it disappeared behind Helen's house. Ash wondered how many first kisses that park had seen, and how many goodbyes.

Someone leaned against the railing next to her. "Hi, stranger." Eddie's teeth were a wide white slash in the darkness. He glanced across the street. "Whatcha you looking at?"

"Nothing, really. Just the night, I guess." His scars seemed less noticeable in the moonlight. Still, she wanted to know his secrets, even as she tried to ignore her own.

He finished his beer in a long, smooth gulp. "It's a great one, isn't it? Terrific party. Everyone's having fun."

"Good." Ash leaned over the railing again, chin propped on one hand. The humidity had finally broken, and now the temperature hovered at a perfect seventy-five degrees. On the breezes that passed through every few minutes, the perfume of Helen's gardenias floated up to them. She took a long breath and drank it all in, wishing she could bottle the night and make it last.

The song on the stereo changed, and Eddie nudged her. "Wanna dance?"

"Here?"

"Why not here?"

Ash hesitated. She didn't need to take center stage with Paradise's favorite son and have someone in the crowd start to wonder why her face looked familiar. Plus, she wasn't sure she trusted herself to put one hand in Eddie's and pretend it didn't take her breath away.

"Ash?" The edge of a tattoo peeked out of a shirtsleeve, and she studied the familiar lines that crossed Eddie's face. She'd memorized them by now, the hairline ones, the thicker one, the patterns they made across his cheeks.

"Okay."

Eddie took her hand. Their fingers met and twisted together, as if they'd done so a hundred times before. She stumbled a little and then found her rhythm, following him as they shuffled in a slow, tight circle. He spun her under his arm, and strong fingers moved across the small of her back. They guided her away and then back to him. They pressed into her palm, burning her skin a little.

The music bled into her veins as they danced around the roof, and for a few minutes, Ashton Kirk forgot everything. She forgot her father's arrest, her mother's plaintive messages, her sister's harsh words. She forgot all her sad feelings, her confusion about Colin. It was just she and Eddie and some silly song. Nothing else mattered, except being in Paradise with someone who wouldn't judge her or expect anything from her. In that instant, she wanted to stay twenty-six, laughing and dancing on rooftops, forever.

The song ended too soon, and they drifted to an awkward stop. Eddie looked down, and Ash glanced away, suddenly self-conscious of her hand in his, of their shoulders brushing in the shadows.

"I should check on the food," she said after a minute.

"Okay." But he didn't drop her hand. "Thanks for the dance."

"Yeah. Thanks." It was all she could manage. Ash slipped back inside to find a corner in which to calm her heart and splash some water on her burning cheeks.

* * *

"Hey, check this out." The voice came from the living room, and when Ash peeked inside, she saw a small knot of people gathered around her television set. The news banner scrolling across the bottom of the screen read, "Kirk Charges Dropped. Two Men Charged in Political Framing of Massachusetts Senator."

Ash dropped the trashcan she held, and beer bottles spilled everywhere. A few people turned toward her, startled, but she didn't care. Pushing through the crowd, she reached for the remote and turned up the volume.

"In a stunning turn of events," the news anchor reported, "all charges originally filed against Senator Randolph Kirk have been dropped. Earlier today, two men came forward and confessed to being hired by a prominent member of the Republican Party to plant cocaine in the senator's vehicle. They also…"

Voices rose, clamoring at the revelation, and Ash lost the rest of the anchor's sentence. By the time she wormed her way close enough to hear, the news had switched over to a segment about a local dog trainer.

"Would never have guessed…

"Told you he was innocent…

"Betcha it turns out to be one of those religious fanatics from…"

Fragments of conversation rose and fell around her, but Ash couldn't make out any of them. In fact, she couldn't follow a single thought beyond the ones racing inside her own head. Her stomach felt as though it might erupt. She reached blindly for a place to sit.

Innocent.

After all this time, her father was innocent. All those weeks, he'd insisted that someone had set him up. *He was right. And no one believed him.* His own family didn't believe him. Ash shook her head. Unshed tears burned in her eyes. Is that why Colin had called last night? Did he already know? She blew out a long breath. Everything had suddenly become more complicated.

"Hey, you okay?" Jen said close to her ear.

Ash jumped, startled. "Did you see it?" One hand waved toward the television screen. Her voice dropped to a whisper. "Did you hear what they said? My father's innocent. Someone set him up."

Her friend stared at her for a long minute. "Yeah, I heard. Now what are you going to do?"

Chapter Fifteen

Ash tied the last bag of garbage and set it near the door. "There. Done."

The clock read after two in the morning. She felt as though she'd been run over by fatigue, but at least the place was clean. The last thing she wanted to do was wake up in an apartment that reeked of stale beer or find a half-naked couple lounging on her living room floor.

Frank and his wife had been the last to leave, about a half-hour ago. She could hear Jen fussing in the bathroom, and she guessed Eddie was somewhere downstairs, hauling boxes of empties onto the porch.

She sank onto the loveseat and let it cradle her. She'd switched shifts with one of the other waitresses at the restaurant, so at least she didn't have to work until the following day. She stretched, and a yawn split her mouth wide. "Think I'll sleep 'til about noon," she said aloud. "Maybe even later."

"Sounds like a good idea." The familiar voice buzzed through her, and she opened her eyes again. She hadn't heard him come in, but there Eddie stood in the doorway, smiling at her. Her heart jumped a little, sending shots of adrenaline into all the wrong places. She'd managed to avoid being alone with him for most of the night, not trusting the tingling in her hands and toes after their dance. But now it sounded like Jen had made her way into the spare bedroom, and nothing stood between Ash and Eddie but a few feet of hardwood.

"Thanks for taking everything downstairs."

"No problem." He sat on the arm of the loveseat. "You need anything else?"

She pretended not to hear the double meaning in his words. Instead, she lifted a hand toward the roof. "Still have to take down the tables and chairs out there. But I guess that can wait until tomorrow."

"I'll do it. Only take a few minutes."

"No, Eddie, really. It can wait."

But he'd already crossed the room and crawled through the window. Ash sighed and followed. She'd much rather wait until she had about ten or twelve hours of sleep, but if he was going to tackle the last of the cleanup, she couldn't very well sit there and watch him.

By the time she made it outside, he'd already collapsed most of the chairs and folded them into stacks of three and four. Two tables still stood, and as Eddie yanked on the legs of one, she found herself watching the way his shirt pulled across his back, the way his hair fell into his eyes, the way his arms flexed and deft hands put things back where they belonged.

Ash made herself look away. Struggling with a few of the chairs, she pulled them toward the window. But the effort exhausted her, and after a minute she leaned against the side of the house to catch her breath.

"You okay?" Eddie glanced over his shoulder.

"Yeah. Just resting." She reached for another chair, but this one sprung open when she touched it, and the next thing she knew, it had pinched her finger in its hinge. Hard.

"Ow! Dammit." Yanking the finger free, she blinked back tears. "That hurt." A blood blister welled up immediately, and she put it to her mouth to try and suck away the pain.

In an instant Eddie was there. He reached for her hand and held it under the weak light that shone out from the kitchen. "Ouch. That's gonna sting for a while."

"No kidding."

He looked at her, concern in his eyes, and suddenly Ash knew she was in trouble. Big, huge, complicated trouble. She felt as if someone had pushed her out of a plane from about a million miles up, and in that moment on the roof, when Eddie held her hand in his, she fell and kept falling, past the point where she knew whether it was right or wrong, to some bottomless, buoyant space where all she wanted to do was stay in his gaze forever.

"Ash? You okay? You want some ice?"

God, she loved the way the words sounded in his mouth. She loved the way he took her nickname and made it sound like no one else ever had. Even the pinpricks of desire Colin had once stirred now seemed like long-dead embers.

"No, I think it's—" She couldn't finish the thought, not with his eyes on her like that. She wanted to pull her hand away, to run the finger under cold water and make the sting go away. But she couldn't move. Eddie's gaze traveled from her hand to her face, and in the next instant there was no more space between them: no floor, no rooftop, barely any air at all.

* * *

Eddie gave up. He couldn't stand there any longer, holding onto Ash's hand and pretending not to notice the desire that rippled back and forth between them like a damn tidal wave. One arm slipped around her, meaning to comfort, but before he knew it, his lips sought out hers. He needed to taste her, to feel her, to fill her with half of what swept through him. For an instant, she hesitated. Then her lips parted, with a sigh that turned into a purr, filling his mouth with want and the promise of things he had no right to even ask.

He pushed Ash's hair from her face and nipped at her lips, her earlobes, the skin at the base of her neck. She jumped a little beneath him, a sizzling electrical wire. His hands moved to her waist, to her hips, to the pliant places along the small of her back. His thumbs moved in circles, stroking tender skin in the spaces where her shirt pulled away from her shorts. He grew hard and pulled her to him, letting her know what she did to him, how she turned him inside out.

"Eddie," she breathed, and in that moment he wanted every part of her, there on the rooftop, beneath the sky. He drank her in, tasting her, pleading, licking, as she melted under his touch. Her hands came up to the back of his neck, nails digging into him. Eddie pulled back long enough to glimpse dark desire in her eyes.

His mouth found her ear, his words a ragged whisper. "God, I want you."

Her response was a lifting of her hips, a pressing against him, heat matching heat. Her tongue wound around his, with quick little pants that made him loose in the knees. Hell, he'd wanted her since the first day he'd run up those stairs and stood in her doorway. He wanted her on the days they argued, on the days he came home too tired to breathe, on the complicated days when one woman or another let herself out of Eddie's apartment. None of them mattered now. He couldn't believe any of them ever had.

Ash was different from any other woman he'd ever met. More intelligent, more secretive, more sensual in the way she moved across a room. More heartbroken, too, though he didn't yet know exactly what or who had devastated her. More confusing, more temperamental, more fragile some days. Was that why she turned him upside down with desire? That crazy combination that he'd never before run across in a woman? Because more than anything, he wanted to wind this amazing creature inside him, possess her, melt into her and lose a little of himself before coming up for air.

"Ash? Are you and Eddie still—oh..."

At Jen's voice in the kitchen, Ash pulled away from him. Through the window, Eddie could see the blonde fishing around in the refrigerator. She held up a hand, as if to block her view. "Sorry. Pretend I was never here, okay?"

But it was too late. One inch between them turned to two and then six. Ash looked up at Eddie, a thousand questions in her eyes that he knew he couldn't answer. *I don't know,* he wanted to say. *I don't know what it means. I don't know what tomorrow brings. All I know is—*

"Stay with me tonight," he whispered. God, if she didn't say yes, he was going to take her right here, neighbors be damned.

She shook her head. One hand lingered on his cheek, on his deepest scar, as she looked from him to Jen and back again. "Eddie, there's so much—"

"Don't." He raised a finger to her lips. "Don't explain. Don't make excuses." He ran a hand through his hair and tried to calm his pounding heart.

"It's just that—"

He kissed her before she could finish, and his last words escaped inside her mouth. "I'll wait, Ash. Okay? For you, I'll wait."

Chapter Sixteen

Ash slept late the next day. She pushed her face under the pillows, trying to ignore the morning sun that streamed through her curtains. Finally, sometime around noon, Jen knocked on her door.

"Ash? You alive in there?"

Alive...

She rolled over. One hand came up to her throat, and she wondered whether Eddie's mouth had left a mark there, a deep strawberry of passion that she could still feel clear down to her toes.

I don't know the last time I felt this alive.

"Yeah," she croaked. "Come on in."

Jen pushed open the door and eased inside. Damp hair swung against her cheeks, and she smelled like soap and shampoo. Her eyes gleamed as she leaned against Ash's dresser.

"So," she began.

Ash pushed herself up. She felt tired, pressed flat, ironed down to little bits of nothing. Though she'd slept for nearly nine hours, her dreams had bounced around, little flickers of Eddie and Colin and her father on the edges of her subconscious. She yawned and drew her hair back from her face.

"Does he kiss as well as he pours tequila shots?"

Her cheeks flamed again. "I don't want to talk about it."

"Why the hell not?"

Ash shrugged and picked at the covers. Because everything else in her life was a total mess right now. Because she couldn't get involved when she'd be leaving town in a couple of months. But mostly because it scared her, the way she felt around Eddie.

"Colin called me the other night," she said instead of answering.

"You're kidding."

"Do I look like I'm kidding?"

"What did he want?"

Ash reached for the bottle of water beside her bed. "I guess to apologize."

"Screw him." Jen narrowed her gaze. "Did you hang up on him? Tell him to go to hell?"

But it wasn't that easy. Ash couldn't just say goodbye to all that. Colin had been her life for three years. She thought he'd be her future, too.

"Ash, don't even tell me you're thinking about taking him back."

"I'm not," she lied.

Jen narrowed her eyes. "Listen, I've got to catch the train. I'll call you later tonight, okay? And we'll talk about it." She gave Ash a quick hug and turned to go. "But let me just say, for the record, that Eddie West is more of a man than Colin will ever be. Screw the pedigree and the money and whatever else you think Colin has to offer you. A hundred of him wouldn't add up to half the personality of that guy living downstairs."

"Yeah, I know," Ash said to the door that closed behind her friend. That was part of the problem.

* * *

Ash finished wiping the last dish and set it in the strainer. After a late lunch of leftover pizza, her stomach had finally calmed down a little. She tuned the radio to a local jazz station and made her way into the living room. Eddie had left one message on her voicemail about an hour ago. She hadn't called him back yet.

What do I say? Do I act like nothing happened? Do I pretend it didn't change anything? Should she call him back? Invite him up?

And if she did, what happened when—or if—he kissed her again? Without Jen to interrupt them, Ash wasn't sure she could trust herself to stop what had started last night.

She shook her head as another thought snuck its way in. What if it didn't mean anything to him? Her fingers tightened around the arm of the couch. She knew as well as anyone how much Eddie liked women. Maybe kissing to him was as natural as breathing. Maybe he'd been swept away by the late hour and too much to drink. Maybe he'd simply wanted to see how she tasted, so he could add her to his list and keep on moving.

Ash tried to quiet the buzzing inside her skull. Pulling a notebook from the end table, she tucked her legs beneath her, meaning to work out a plan. That was how she'd always tackled the tough problems, back in school. Lay everything out on paper, and then sort out a solution.

She found a pencil and made two columns. She wrote "Eddie" on top of one and "Colin" headed the other. A solid line split the two in half. *Now just be objective. Just come up with a list, something measurable, so you can balance one against the other and—*

Someone knocked on her door.

The pencil dropped from her fingers and rolled beneath the couch.

"Ash?"

Eddie. Desire sang inside her veins. "Just a minute." She stuffed the notebook between two cushions and went to the door. Opening it, she blurted a breathless, "Hi."

The way he looked down at her, with sleep-wrinkles lining the edge of his face and a toothpaste smile, sent her mind reeling all over again. "Hi, yourself."

He didn't try to kiss her, or even touch her. He just stood there and looked, the way he had the very first day he moved in. "You feeling okay?"

She wasn't sure how to answer that. "Sure. You?"

He leaned in the doorway. "There's something I need to tell you."

She went cold. "That doesn't sound good."

"Can I come in?"

"Sure." She pushed the door wider, certain by his serious tone that he meant to set the record straight. He'd say last night had been a mistake. He'd tell her he was involved with someone else. Or that he was getting back together with Cass.

Ash bit her bottom lip and sat down on the couch. Stuffing her hands beneath her thighs, so they wouldn't betray her by reaching over to touch him, she waited.

"I know we've only been living here a few weeks."

True.

"And I know you think I'm the kind of guy who sleeps around, or who flirts with lots of women, but doesn't mean anything by it."

She found herself holding her breath. "I don't think that."

"Sure you do."

Ash looked at her lap until he reached over and stroked her cheek with his thumb. "I couldn't sleep last night," he confessed.

Her heart sped up a little.

"I thought... there's so much I don't even know about this woman."

Guilt replaced giddiness inside Ash's chest. She didn't mean to keep secrets from Eddie. Really, she didn't. She just wouldn't know where to begin to tell him the truth.

"But then, there are things you don't know about me, either. Things that might help you understand."

She looked up at the odd tone in his voice. "What things?"

Eddie looked past her, over her head, to a shadow that might have danced on the wall behind her. "When I was eight years old, my mom got cancer."

"Oh, Eddie... I'm so sorry." The words left her mouth and bounced like hollow cylinders around the room. *How much we hide, wrap close to the skin.* Just when it seemed she knew her housemate, more layers of him peeled away, so that each time she saw him, a new Eddie emerged.

"She was just thirty-two," he went on. "God, it was scary, especially for a little kid. I couldn't understand what was happening. Everyone else's mom came to Open House and baked cookies for snack time and rode on the bus with us to the zoo. Mine just changed from this happy person who smiled all the time to a skeleton that lay on our couch in the living room and slept. Fourth grade? I can't tell you a thing about it. I spent all my time at the hospital visiting my mom, or taking care of my little brother and sister at home."

"I didn't know you had siblings," Ash interrupted. He'd never mentioned them, and only one picture of Eddie, at his high school graduation with both parents, stood in a frame on his television downstairs.

His face clouded. "Kelly's eighteen. Just finished high school. And my brother Cal..." He left the sentence unfinished.

"But after awhile, she got better, like the huge miracle everyone had prayed for. She got better, and went into remission, and things were great then. My dad was in a good mood, and even Kelly and Cal didn't annoy me so much. I was happy, really happy, you know?"

Ash nodded.

"I thought, if only things stay just like this, with my mom healthy and all of us getting along, then I couldn't ever want anything else." Eddie took a long breath. "For a long time, I really was that happy." His hair fell over his eyes as he looked down at his lap

"Then Cal died in a car accident."

"Oh, Eddie." My God, how much sorrow could one soul take? Ash looked again at her housemate, and this time she saw pain deep and lasting. *He does know what it means to have a family ripped apart. Maybe he'd understand about mine, after all.* Little pieces of the reserve inside her began to crack apart.

"It was three years ago. We were driving home from the movies, and Cal was laughing over some stupid joke he'd heard in school," Eddie continued. "He was seventeen, you know, trying to act all grown up, but still a stupid kid, too big for his shoes and tripping over his feet."

A smile flashed onto his face but was gone in an instant.

"I was driving, and we were just a couple of blocks from home when this car ran a red light, ran right into us without even slowing down. I tried to stop, but everything happened so fast...and I wasn't looking the way I usually do. I was watching Cal tell the joke and thinking how cool he was going to be when he got a little older. I'd always thought he was a dork, but he was starting to get it. He was starting to turn into a man." Eddie swallowed as if something in his throat hurt him. "He would have been such a good man."

His next words came out in a sob. "The light was green, my way. It wasn't red, or even yellow. It was green. I know it was, because I still see it every night in my sleep." He squeezed the bridge of his nose, but two tears spilled over his fingers before he could stop them.

"Eddie, you don't have to..." But he waved away her words with a damp hand. "It was a drunk driver, so bombed that he never even remembered hitting us. Ran into Cal's side of the car, square on. Docs said he never felt anything, died on impact. I hope so. 'Cause all I thought about after that was what if we'd gone to the late show, or what if we'd stopped for a burger the way Cal wanted to? What if that guy hadn't left the bar when he did?" Eddie's voice began to shake a little.

"Sometimes I think Cal's lucky. At least he's free. I deal with it every day. Every fuckin' day."

For a few minutes, his ragged breaths were the only sound in the apartment. Ash didn't move. Didn't speak. She didn't even trust herself to reach out to him in comfort.

Eddie raised a hand and traced the line along his jawbone. "So yeah, that's what the scars are from. Plastic surgery only does so much. The doctor said he could have gotten rid of this one..." He touched his cheek gently. "But I wanted it. I wanted to remember."

He stopped talking and sat there for a long time with his eyes closed.

You didn't need to tell me all this, Ash wanted to say. *I didn't need to know.* Yet she knew why the words had spilled from him the minute he'd sat down next to her. It was easy for them. They could sit and not say anything special. They didn't have to be funny, or flirty, or witty, or even kind. They could just be...whatever they wanted. The realization scared the hell out of her.

When he spoke again, Eddie looked at her with such fierce affection that her heart swooped. "But I'm happy now, Ash, really happy, for the first time in I can't remember how long." He shook his head. "After the accident, my life went to shit. I drank too much. I took six months off from work and slept all day. I dated the wrong women just to fill up the nights. I blamed myself for Cal's death. Still do. Most days, to be honest, I wished I were dead too."

He stopped and took a breath. "Then I moved in here, and met you, and everything changed." His hand moved over hers in soft circles, until she felt as though her insides might float away.

"It's different with you, Ash. It's like I don't have to pretend."

"Eddie, I—"

"I know you're only here for the summer." He pulled her close, wrapping both arms around her and murmuring into her hair. "I know that. But Boston isn't that far away." His lips moved against her temple. "Maybe we could give it a try. Maybe we could—"

He twisted a little. "What am I sitting on?"

Oh, no. Ash reached to grab the notebook, but Eddie had already pulled it from between the cushions. He smoothed its wrinkled top page and glanced down. "What is...?" His words fell away. When he looked up again, something had fallen across his face, a chilly pall that stole all warmth from his expression.

"Who's Colin?"

"Eddie, it's nothing. No one." She took the notebook and tossed it onto the floor.

"Your ex-boyfriend? The one you never talk about?"

She waved a hand. "Yeah. But that's over with. He doesn't matter." She tried to run her fingers across Eddie's face and calm the irritation growing there.

"Why are you making lists about him? About him and me?"

"It's nothing. It's just..." How could she explain? "It's something I do sometimes, to sort things out."

"What needs sorting out? Are you still in love with him?"

"No. But it's complicated."

"I thought you said it was over."

"It is." *And it isn't.*

His voice softened then. "Then tell me about it. About him. Let me in, Ash. For once."

"There's nothing to tell," she whispered. "Really."

Eddie punched the arm of the loveseat. "I sit here and tell you all about the accident that ripped my life in half, all about the brother I lost, and you can't even talk to me about your ex? What is it? You don't trust me?" With every word, his voice raised, until he was shouting.

"That's not it," Ash began. "I just..." *I can't get into it,* she wanted to say. *I can't tell you about Colin without telling you about my father. And I can't tell you about my father without telling you my real name. And then you'll know I've been lying to you all along.*

Eddie stared at her for another minute. Then he shot to a stand. "If you can't trust me, there's no way this will work. Ever."

Tears bubbled up to the surface, and Ash looked away in case they fell. She couldn't think of a single thing to say.

"You know, I'm not stupid. I know you came to Paradise because something chased you out of Boston. I know you're running away from something. Or someone." His voice shook. "And I don't care. I've never pushed. But if you can't even begin to tell me about it—"

Eddie's voice broke, and he didn't finish, just retraced his steps to the front door and shut it behind him.

That was what happened when you let yourself get involved, Ash thought. Her chest tightened. She never should have kissed him. She never should have become friends with him in the first place.

But it was too late for that, and she knew it. She stared at her door, willing it open again. Suddenly, she wanted to confess everything. She wanted to look into those dark eyes and know Eddie didn't care where she came from or who she really was. She wanted to feel his mouth on hers again. She wanted him to fold his arms around her and tell her everything would be okay.

But she didn't know if it would be.

Chapter Seventeen

Twenty-four hours of heartless rain poured down. It soaked the roof and seeped into Ash's bedroom in the form of dreary dampness. She rearranged her furniture. She took all the recyclables to the store, careful to avoid looking at Eddie's door on the way there and back. She rearranged her CD collection. She drove all the way to Burnt Hills, a leftover hippie colony past Silver Creek rumored to have the best hummus in the state.

Finally, she gave in and called her mother.

"Ashton!" Mamie Kirk's voice wobbled. "Where have you been?"

"I'm sorry." She curled into a ball on the loveseat and stared at the ceiling. "It's just...I needed to take a break from things back home. It was getting a little crazy." *Getting crazy? Already way beyond, if you want the truth.*

"Jess said you're subletting a place in New Hampshire?" Doubt crept into her mother's voice and hung there, waiting for Ash to correct her, to say that no, Jess was wrong, she wouldn't do something so un-Kirk-like.

"Mm hmm," Ash said instead.

"You've heard about your father? About the charges being dropped?"

"Yes."

"We'd like to make a statement to the press," she went on when Ash didn't. "At the house on Martha's Vineyard. The secretary of state will be there next week, and we're planning on joining him and his wife for a few days."

God, no. Ash squeezed her eyes shut. Less than three months away from that life, and it already seemed foreign to her, as if she'd never lived it at all.

"So will you be there?"

"I don't think I can make it."

"Ash, your father needs all of us together. As a family. You know the nomination is—"

"I know. The most important thing in his life right now." *And that's why he needs the shiny, happy faces of his wife and daughters with him when the cameras start snapping.*

"The thing is, I'm working," she said. "I'm not sure I can get away."

Mamie didn't answer, a quick intake of breath the only indication that she'd heard. "Well...what do you mean, exactly? You're not...you haven't taken a position with another firm, have you? Not up there?"

Oh, how that would complicate things. Ash almost smiled. She could just picture the headline: "Youngest Kirk daughter turns down prestigious job in Boston only to slum in the hills of New Hampshire." Part of her wanted to tell her mother just where she spent her working hours. *It's a jazz club in a blue-collar town. I serve people food and then clean up after them. Want me to issue a statement to the press about that?* But she kept her mouth shut.

"We'll be at the Vineyard the whole week," her mother said. "I'm sure you can take some time off." She paused. "Colin asked if he can join us."

"What?" Ash sat straight up. "No. No way." How dare he try to weasel his way back into her life? That's what the phone call was all about. He didn't miss her. He missed the Kirk name. He missed the reputation. Her cheeks burned with anger. "Forget it."

"Ash, please—"

"He broke up with me, Mom. Did you know that? That Colin dumped me right after everything happened with Dad? That he was sleeping with someone else?"

"No, I didn't. I..." Her mother choked off into silence.

"Tell Dad I'm sorry," Ash said. "I wish I could be there. I do. But I can't." She couldn't play that charade, shrug that life on again like a skin that just slipped off for a few weeks. It wasn't that easy.

"I'm sorry you feel that way." Mamie hiccupped, but Ash could hear her smoothing her voice, ratcheting down any emotion that might betray her. The way she always did. The way she probably always would.

"I'll have Jess or Anne call you next week," she went on, as if Ash hadn't refused to join them at the Kirk vacation home but simply said she needed to check her calendar. "Maybe you can find some time to work us in."

"Mom, listen. It's not that I don't want to be there for Dad. I just..."

"I know. You have a life of your own, and you want to live it. I understand that."

Ash weakened a little.

"But your father needs your support. Is that too much to ask?"

Ash didn't answer. She didn't know. And when her mother hung up a moment later, all she really knew was that she felt exhausted beyond belief, squeezed tight and wrung out, like laundry left too long in the rain.

* * *

"Evenin', boss." J.T. flashed Ash a smile as she stepped inside Blues and Booze. The stupid umbrella she'd grabbed from her car had lasted exactly thirty seconds before it pulled itself inside out and went twisting down the sidewalk away from her.

She ignored his greeting and stomped through the bar, checking the orders and the cash register before making her way to the kitchen.

"Well, somebody's got her panties in a knot," she heard behind her. One of the guys at the bar, she supposed. Probably Jackson Todd. Or maybe Tyler Mulligan. J.T.'s cronies often hung out after their shifts at the cheese factory, slurping down a few beers before going home to their wives.

She didn't bother to turn around. *Get it together, Ash. A bad mood isn't going to get you anywhere. It's not their fault your life is a total mess right now. You have work to do. So do it.* She grabbed a clipboard and pulled open the coolers in the back, making notes as she went down each shelf. "More apple pie, more double-chocolate torte, still enough cheesecake..."

"Ash?" Lacey waltzed into the kitchen. "Carla just called. Said she can't make it tonight. Car trouble or something."

"You're kidding." Their newest waitress, a single mother of two, had called in late three times in the last week. Ash really needed to tell Marty to get rid of her. If they couldn't depend on Carla, she might as well look somewhere else for a job. Ash would pick up extra shifts if she had to.

Lacey started making salads, draping them loosely with plastic wrap and storing them in the refrigerator. "Sorry."

Ash shrugged. "We'll deal. Rain might keep people away, anyway."

"Remember that Ladies' Day idea you were talking about?" Lacey asked. She dumped out the afternoon's coffee and started another pot.

Ash nodded. She'd thought about opening the restaurant on Sunday afternoons, offering specials for Paradise's wives and girlfriends whose men spent the day staring at eight straight hours of baseball. Maybe introduce a vegetarian dish or two. Maybe get one of the local salons to offer manicures. She didn't know any of the girls who worked in Hair Heaven or Nails and Tails, but she supposed she could ask around.

Ash bit her bottom lip as a thought snuck its way in. That wasn't exactly true, was it? She knew Cass worked at one of the salons in Paradise.

"Hi yourself, Cassandra. What the hell are you doing here?"

"Stopping by to say hi, that's all...It's been a while. You haven't stopped by the salon..."

Cassandra. And Eddie. That thought hurt.

"Ash?"

"Sorry." She jumped, and the pencil slipped from her fingers. "What?"

Lacey gave her a funny look. "I was talking to my housemates about it. They think the Sunday thing's a great idea. They'd definitely come."

"Oh. Well, good. Maybe I'll mention it to Marty, see what he thinks."

Lacey nodded and backed through the swinging door. "Let me know if I can help. I wouldn't mind picking up another shift."

Ash straightened her shirt and grabbed a fresh stack of order slips. Deep down, she hoped the rain brought people in today, rather than kept them away. That way she could keep her mind on juggling trays instead of botched kisses and awkward telephone conversations she didn't know how to sort out. She spent another ten minutes sorting through napkins and tablecloths in the back. Then she filled two pitchers of ice water and walked into the dining room.

"Could we have some menus?"

"I asked for Absolut, not Stoli."

"I thought tonight's special was going to be chicken."

Ash stopped and stared. Three-quarters of the restaurant was packed with people escaping the storm.

"Can you believe this?" Lacey whizzed by on her way to the kitchen. "I've never seen a night like this."

Neither had Ash.

"Came in for the meatloaf," June Frisbie confided, as she stopped by the elderly woman's table. "Saw it on the specials board outside and couldn't resist."

"Glad to hear it," Ash said. "Don't know if there's enough back there for everyone, but I'll make sure to set aside an extra-large serving for you." She bent closer and aimed her voice at the woman's hearing aid. "Make sure to save some for Dobber and Jones."

The woman broke out in a huge smile at the mention of her two beloved poodles. "Oh, I will." She patted Ash on the wrist. "Dear, you're the best thing that's happened to this place since Marty took it over. I hope you'll be staying a while."

Ash moved on without answering.

"Ash!" A heavyset man dressed in head-to-toe camouflage waved her over.

"Hi, guys." She nodded a hello to the three farmers, portly and red-cheeked. "Nice to see you." She glanced at their empty table. "Need a pitcher of Bud?"

The men nodded in unison. "Better make it two."

"Coming right up."

She headed for the bar and checked in with J.T. "What do you need?"

"Another set of hands would be nice."

She cracked a smile. "Wish I could." But she slipped behind the bar and started pouring drinks and filling pitchers. "Give you a few minutes, anyway."

Lacey flashed back to the bar, slim legs trotting faster than Ash had ever seen them move. The young girl loaded up a tray, grabbed some cocktail napkins, and took off again.

"She's working her tail off tonight," Ash noted, glad to see it.

"Nice tail it is, too," one of the guys at the bar guffawed.

Ash pointed a finger in his direction. "Watch it," she said with a serious squint of the eyes. She recognized him but couldn't come up with a name. *Give me another hour and I'll remember it for the rest of the summer.* Once again, she was glad the photographic memory that had served her so well in college was coming in handy.

"Ash?" The new Blues and Booze hostess, a meek woman of forty, shuffled over. Behind her, a crowd of people jostled for space in the restaurant's narrow lobby. "We just got a party of twelve. Can we take them?"

"Let me see." She surveyed the dining room. "I think Gus Masterson'll move if I ask him to, and the Wallaces just decided they're getting take-out instead of staying, so we'll push those tables together and..."

* * *

"There." Three hours later, Ash set down the bill for table nineteen and exhaled. Her feet ached. Her throat was raw. Her shirt stuck to her lower back. Her hair had fallen from its ponytail and hung around her face. She rolled her neck. Well, at least the rush had kept her mind off anything except running orders, replacing napkins, and filling empty glasses. What next? She looked around for a table to clear, a new party to seat. But the room was quiet. Finally.

She took a few minutes to drink a tall glass of water and then found Lacey in the kitchen. "Are we actually finished?"

The girl smiled. Her eyes shone with fatigue. "I think so. God, I never saw such a rush."

"Me either."

Lacey pulled a wad of bills from her pocket. "Definitely over a hundred."

"Good for you." Ash sagged against the salad bar, exhausted.

Lacey eyed her. "You okay? You were running like crazy tonight, too."

"Tell me about it."

The college student pulled off her apron and headed for the door. "You're good at this, you know. I mean, I know you're probably not staying around Paradise forever, but still..." She shrugged. "You'd be good at running a restaurant. If you ever wanted to."

Ash didn't say anything. She wasn't sure how she felt about that. She did like being in charge. She liked the social part of the job. And there was a lot less stress involved in keeping customers happy than memorizing cases or prepping briefs, even on a night like tonight. But a lifetime of it? She thought she'd probably go a little stir-crazy.

"You can head home, Lace," she said without answering the girl's question. She glanced at the time clock. Almost nine on a Tuesday, and Eddie hadn't stopped in. He always came in on Tuesdays after work. Always, since the second day she'd worked there.

But could she blame him for staying away? He hadn't called or come upstairs since their fight, over twenty-four hours earlier. She thought again of the anger in his voice, the disappointment in his gaze, as he waited for her to talk about Colin. About her past. About her family.

He had no idea what he was asking her. Something clutched inside her chest, and she bent over in pain.

"Ash? You okay?"

"Yeah," she said, waiting for the feeling to pass. "Just a cramp. I'll be fine."

Eddie. Mom. Dad. The Vineyard. Blues and Booze. Ash stared at her toes. How had her life become this complicated? Four months ago, she'd been a regular law student, with a regular boyfriend and a regular job awaiting her. Today she had none of that. She had nothing to count on, no predictability beyond her weekly shift schedule. Most mornings, she didn't even know the woman who stared back at her from the mirror.

How on earth had she gotten herself so far away from her life as a Kirk? And where was she headed from here?

Chapter Eighteen

The rain broke around eleven, and by the time Ash left the restaurant a little after midnight, the moon had begun to sneak its way through the clouds.

It changes in an instant. She stepped over puddles that caught the reflection of the trees lining the parking lot. One minute everything was dreary, and the next there was light every place she looked. She sighed and sank into her car without turning it on. *Or the other way around. Bright to black in a heartbeat.*

He hadn't shown. She'd waited all night for Eddie to walk through the front door, almost certain he'd come. Certain he felt the same way she did, shaken up and fizzy, but wanting to hold on to whatever had started up on the porch roof two nights ago. Maybe this time she was wrong. With leaden fingers, Ash turned the key in the ignition. No more problems with her car, that was for sure. Since Eddie had worked his magic on it, it hadn't so much as purred the wrong way.

"I, on the other hand..." she said aloud. She managed to break things before they even showed signs of cracking.

She pulled out of the lot and made a left instead of a right. She didn't want to go home. Not right away. Not if it meant looking at Eddie's closed door and wanting more than anything to knock and tell him her secrets. Maybe he wouldn't think she was crazy. Maybe he wouldn't care that she'd lied to him about her name. Maybe he would understand if she told him why.

And maybe he wouldn't.

Ash swung into a new development on the edge of town, slowing as she passed the bi-level homes. She wondered who lay sleeping inside them. Newlyweds? Single moms trying to keep it all together? Happy families with perfect lives? Or hardworking laborers trying to piece together a living the way their parents and grandparents had? She rolled down the windows and fresh air poured inside.

Barely a sound filled the night air. Just the hum of air conditioners and the occasional chirp of a restless bird carried through the evening. She imagined for a moment the constant buzz of the city —the mix of cars and voices and music from dance clubs—that would fill the streets of Boston at that hour. She didn't miss it. Not one bit.

At the end of the cul-de-sac, she swung her VW in a slow circle. She couldn't stay in Paradise. It wasn't her home. She had no ties here, not really. But the thought of joining the rest of her family on Martha's Vineyard next weekend turned her stomach. The thought of seeing Colin again tied her up in knots. Not there, not here. Where did she belong?

A door opened suddenly, and a beam of light speckled one of the driveways to her right. A black Lab emerged, sniffing the air. It meandered down the lawn and flopped onto its back. Legs straight up, it rolled from side to side on the wet grass. Ash could see its tongue lolling from its mouth.

"Angus!" The voice was a hiss in the darkness. "Stop that!" Into the frame of light waddled a woman so pregnant she looked as though she might fall over.

Ash smiled. Dottie Warren stopped into the restaurant once in a while after her shift at the Post Office. "I told Mick I didn't need to do desk duty," she'd told Ash over a vanilla milkshake and french fries last week. "Told him I could still deliver on the route. Christ, I been through this three times already. But you know how men are. Always think they know what's best..."

Ash raised a hand to wave, though she knew the woman couldn't see her. Still, as she drove by, she thought Dottie took an extra look at her car, tucking away the color and the silhouette of its driver. After a moment, the dog peed and trotted back inside. Dottie shut the door, and the outside light turned off again. Ash grinned. Tomorrow or the next day, she knew, the woman would amble into the restaurant and ask Ash what she was doing on Miller's Circle after midnight.

No secrets in this town. You know that. The minute you tell Eddie who you are, word will spread. Everyone will know. And everything will change. She yanked the rubber band from her ponytail and let her hair fall to her shoulders. The breeze picked up as she pulled away from the stop sign and gave the car some gas.

"Well, so what if it does?" She couldn't pretend anymore. She was tired of living a secret. It was too damn hard. Ash tightened her fingers around the steering wheel. She had to make things right.

"I'm going to tell him everything." And they would take it from there.

She bit her bottom lip and hoped he would still look at her the same way afterwards. She hoped he would still wrap those strong arms around her, still press his lips against hers, and still pull her into his embrace like there was nowhere else he wanted to be.

* * *

It was after one by the time she killed the engine in front of the house. Ash dragged herself up the sidewalk. *Do I see if he's still up? Or do I wait until tomorrow? I want—* She didn't know what she wanted. That was the problem.

She pushed open the front door, which he'd left unlocked. The porch light still burned, too. All good signs. Ash stood in the foyer and studied the stairs, working up the nerve to knock on Eddie's door. She took one step forward, raised her hand, then glanced down at herself and realized she probably smelled like the kitchen of Blues and Booze. Wrinkling her nose, she stepped back again.

Tomorrow, when I've had a shower and some sleep and we can talk about this rationally.

But when was the last time she'd done anything rationally when it came to Eddie West? That was what worked, what made him – and her, when she was around him – different. Better. Her hand reached up and knocked before she could stop it. "Eddie?"

She heard nothing for a minute. Her stomach clenched. What if he was in there with someone? What if he'd completely changed his mind? She guessed there were half a dozen women in Paradise who'd be more than happy to warm his bed and soothe his wounded ego.

Ash traced a crack on the floor with one toe. She knocked once more and waited a long thirty seconds. Well, if he was home, he wasn't answering. It would have to wait until tomorrow after all. She turned to go.

"Ash?"

She'd almost made it to the stairs by the time his door swung open. She turned around, heart in her throat. Eddie stood on the threshold, bare-chested and dozy-eyed. He wore a pair of cut-off sweats and nothing else.

She forgot how to breathe.

"What time is it?"

"Late. I'm sorry." The words came out in a rush. "I shouldn't have—were you sleeping?"

He shook his head and ran a hand through his hair, standing it up on end. "Watching TV." He paused for a moment, then pushed the door open all the way. "Want to come in?"

"Okay."

The living room smelled of him, of that complicated scent she associated with baseball games and late nights on the porch and winks in the bar as he sat and watched her count tips. Ash stopped near the recliner and looked around. The kitten, now a few pounds rounder in the belly, slept on a towel Eddie had tucked into a cardboard box.

"You ever give it a name?"

He closed the door and stepped beside her, breathing the words into her ear. "Call 'im Tiny. Seems to like it."

She smiled. "It fits him."

He sat on the edge of the couch. "So?"

"I'm sorry." Second time in less than five minutes. Why didn't she just apologize her way into tomorrow? But there didn't seem to be any other words to fit the enormity of what she needed to say.

"Sit." Eddie cocked his head at her. "Stop being so goddamned nervous and tell me what's going on."

"It's complicated." She worked her way toward him.

"So start with something small." He leaned back as she edged onto the couch. "Start with—I don't know. Why you decided to leave Boston."

Ash laughed. "I wouldn't call that something small." That was the biggest part of what she need to say. And the hardest.

He didn't say anything, didn't press, didn't keep questioning. He just studied her with his intent gaze, until she felt sure he'd stripped off every last stitch of clothing she wore and saw through to the heart that beat erratically under her skin.

One hand worked its way across the cushion until it rested on his bare leg. "What happened the other night..." she began.

"Was nice. Was good. Should happen a lot more."

She let out a long breath. "Yeah."

Eddie's hand reached for hers. Ash let her gaze move across his chest, over the pale fuzz that spread there. Up to the tattoo on his triceps. Over to his square chin, that bobbed when he spoke too fast or got too excited. Down, just for an instant, to the waistband of the cut-offs that dipped below his navel. Then up, where blue eyes met hers and a mouth looked as though it waited for her to make up her mind.

"There's so much I need to tell you."

"Can it wait?" Eddie pulled her toward him, working his hand from hers. He slipped his arm around her waist and drew her across the cushions, so that her curves melted into his. "Because I am so damn crazy about you that all I want to do is this." He caught her mouth with his, tongue opening her lips and seeking, teasing, making her ache. "And this." His hand moved inside her shirt, burning her skin everywhere he touched it.

"Eddie..." But there was nothing she wanted to say. Nothing she wanted to explain. All that could wait. A dizzying rush of desire came over her, so strong and so sudden that she felt as though all the air had been sucked out of the room.

His mouth moved to her neck. Her earlobe. Then down. Inch by inch he tasted her, achingly slow, taking his time. One hand moved to the small of her back. She heard a quick breath, a gasp of pleasure, and realized seconds later that she'd made the sounds.

In agonizing layers Eddie peeled it all away: her T-shirt, her bra, her shorts, the lacy pink panties she'd chosen carefully that morning, hoping and not hoping that this moment might unfold. Then he moved over her, and she reached for him, easing down the cut-off sweats that remained between them until there was nothing at all but skin upon skin and desire filling the room from ceiling to floor.

*　*　*

It was nothing like being with Colin. It wasn't like anything Ash had experienced with anyone, ever before, this movement that carried her far from the house on Lycian Street, out over the treetops and to some distant island where all she could feel were the waves beneath her and the amazing sun above her.

Behind her eyelids fifty different colors blended together, sparklers of light that took her breath away. Eddie settled her on the couch, and she was glad they didn't move to the bedroom. She wouldn't have made it that far. She wanted him *now*, needed his hands and mouth on her *now*, bringing her to the edge until she whimpered with pleasure. She dug her fingers into his arms as he moved above her, felt the skin of his back, tasted the salt of his neck, etched the burn of his beard into her memory.

He murmured into her temple and stroked the edge of her collarbone. And when she pulled back to look at him, she saw such tenderness in his gaze that she thought she might weep. Her mouth fell onto his shoulder, teeth burying themselves in the soft skin there because it was all she could do to keep from crying out.

"God, I want you, Ash. So much."

She closed her eyes as he rose toward her, into her, faster and faster, bringing her with him until she came, tightening around him. She bit her lip so hard she tasted blood, and waves of pleasure raised gooseflesh along every inch of her skin. He pulled back the tiniest bit to look at her, focus his gaze squarely on hers. But he didn't stop moving, and after a moment he gathered her closer, let her feel him inside her, the perfect dance that took her orgasm and teased it into another, and then a third. In muted tones, Ash cried out, begging Eddie to stop, to go on, to lose himself inside her. Until he did.

Chapter Nineteen

Eddie slept better than he had in months—in years, really. At one point he woke, as early morning sunlight slipped through his bedroom window. Outside, the garbage truck dumped buckets of recyclables, shattering glass and clanking tin cans against cement. A car horn beeped. The church downtown struck the hour. He ran a hand across his chest, savoring the heaviness of morning-after satisfaction, though it had never before been so solid, so comforting.

He moved one foot and touched Ash's warm, sleek skin next to his. *She's here. I didn't dream it.* He turned over with that lazy pleasure of knowing there was nowhere else he needed to be, no work commitments to fulfill, no bad dreams to outrun. Wrapping one arm around her, he pulled her into him, still naked. He curved around her. Her spine melted into him, her breathing deepened, and even in half sleep he felt himself rise against her. Something moved at the bottom of the bed, and after a moment, he felt the brush of kitten fur against his bare shoulder. Tiny settled into the sheets, one paw patting at him, until the cat fell asleep too. Its purr rumbled to a quiet snore.

Eddie closed his eyes. The perfect morning. He wished all of them could be like this.

* * *

"Eddie?"

He swam up from dreams at the sound of her voice.

"Eddie." This time she nudged him, pressed a warm knee against his side and murmured the word into his ear.

He rolled over and opened one eye. "Morning."

Ash smiled. Her hair, loose and messy, fell over her forehead. "Good morning yourself." She glanced toward the living room. "You hear that?"

He shook his head and propped himself up on one elbow. One hand smoothed its way over her hips, rising to soft curves under the sheets.

"It sounded like a knock."

Eddie shrugged and bent to kiss the tip of her nose. "Didn't hear anything." The sheets fell away from them, and he moved his hands across the ridges of her collarbone. Then down. He was ready for round two, no doubt about it. Usually for him, the morning after meant quick trips to the bathroom, fumbling for clothes, awkward joking about breakfast. Not this time. He felt no rush, no wondering, no moment of second thought. With Ash, it felt as though they'd done this a hundred times.

She shifted under his touch, and her eyes closed. Her breath hitched. He leaned in to taste the curve of her breast and stopped. There it was, a polite knocking from about a hundred feet away. Maybe closer. Definitely outside number two Lycian Street.

"Probably a salesman," he murmured. "Or some kid selling candy."

Ash laughed beneath him. "You're not in the mood for Girl Scout cookies this morning?"

"Mmm...no. But I can tell you what I am in the mood for."

"Hello?" This time a voice accompanied the knocking. A male voice Eddie didn't recognize.

Ash sat up, and the covers fell from her shoulders. All color drained from her face.

"What's wrong?"

She didn't speak. She only raised both hands to her chest and clutched at her skin as if to shut him out. In slow motion she turned in the direction of the voice, and when she looked back at Eddie, something in her eyes had changed.

A pause. Some footsteps. Then the knocking came again, closer this time. Eddie realized that someone— Helen?—had let the stranger inside their foyer, and now he stood directly outside Eddie's apartment door.

"You know who it is?" He stared at Ash, who was edging her way out of bed.

"Um..." She didn't answer, just grabbed a T-shirt from the fresh stack in his laundry basket and pulled it over her head. The logo of Frank's Imports, faded and peeling, landed above her ribs. The fraying edge came down below the swell of her ass. Barely.

The knocking continued. "Hello? Is anyone there?"

Eddie swung his feet over the bed. What the hell was going on?

"Don't answer it." Ash hovered by the bedroom door, chewing at a fingernail.

"Why not?" He yanked on a pair of boxer shorts and headed for the living room. "The guy already woke me up." Irritated, he ran a rough hand across his chin. Damn. He'd been meaning to trim the goatee for a while now. Today, maybe. His hair, too long as well, fell across his eyes.

"Eddie."

He turned to see Ash still frozen in his doorway. Pain etched a line from her brows to her down-turned mouth. "I'm sorry." It was all she said, a quiet apology. Yet days later, it would be the only thing Eddie could hear echoing in his skull, the only thing he could remember of the moment before everything changed, the moment before he opened the door and saw Senator Randolph Kirk standing outside.

*　*　*

"I'm sorry to bother you."

From the bedroom, Ash heard the voice again. Smooth, kind, polished through years of public service. She closed her eyes and tried to ignore the pain seizing up inside her. How had he found her? Why had he come?

"You...you're Senator Kirk, right?"

"Randolph. Please."

Ash leaned against the wall and entertained the idea of going out Eddie's back window. She could climb outside, sneak down the block, maybe stall for a couple of hours in the coffee shop. She looked down at herself. *Oh, yeah? In what? Eddie's shirt?* The rest of her clothes lay somewhere out in the living room, still tossed on the floor. In plain sight. *Oh, God.*

"I'm looking for my daughter. Ashton." Pause. "I understand she may be staying in the neighborhood for the summer, and..."

"Sir, I don't think I can help you." Politeness coated Eddie's words. Ash could have cried. "I don't know her."

Go out there. You can't hide in Eddie's bedroom forever. You can't pretend this isn't happening. But maybe she could. Maybe Eddie would steer her father in a different direction.

"This is her picture," her father went on. "A few people in the grocery store said they've seen her. Said she might be working at a restaurant here in town. And the woman across the street—"

"I don't think..." Eddie stopped.

In her mind's eye, Ash saw him study the picture. Saw him do a double take and look closer. Saw the corners of his mouth twitch. Imagined that bile rose in the back of his throat as he looked at an image of the woman he'd just spent the night with, the woman who had lived upstairs, and lied to him, all summer long. She forced herself to walk down the hall.

"You can stop looking," she said. "I'm here."

Her father stood in the open doorway, one hand in the pocket of his pressed suit pants, the other absently picking at a buttonhole in his sports coat. He looked the same as always. Poised and confident. Taller than the average man, but not haughty even though he looked down on just about everyone.

"Ashton!" His gaze shifted as she walked into the living room, and she saw him take in the T-shirt she wore and her bare legs beneath it. He looked from her to Eddie and back again. He swallowed, a small motion that anyone else might have missed. But she saw it and knew exactly what it meant. Disappointment. Disapproval.

Then he smiled, and it was true and fatherly, the way she remembered. "It's good to see you."

Eddie frowned. "You're...I don't...What's going on here?" He stared at Ash and pushed the picture back at her father. "Why are you here?"

She wasn't sure who he meant, her or her father. Neither one answered.

"Ash?"

Finally she drew a breath. "Yes. He's my father," she whispered. "I'm sorry I didn't tell you."

Eddie shook his head. "I don't get it. Who are you? What's your real name?"

"I'll give you two a minute," Senator Kirk said, and slipped back into the foyer. The door clicked shut.

Ash wound the edge of Eddie's T-shirt around her fingers.

"You're Senator Kirk's daughter?"

She nodded.

"Are you fucking kidding? Why didn't you tell me?" Eddie's voice turned thick.

"I didn't know how."

He took her by the shoulders, squaring her off and forcing her to meet his gaze. "Why the hell not?" He shook his head. "Jesus, what else haven't you told me? Is it all a lie? Law school? Breaking up with your boyfriend? Every damn thing?"

Her tongue moved inside her mouth, searching for words. He spun away from her. Facing the windows, he laced his hands behind his head. "Just leave, Ash. Or Ashton. Or whatever your name really is."

"Eddie, please. I'll tell you. I'll explain everything." Ash sucked in a breath and held it.

But he didn't say anything, just shook his head again. The muscles in his back drew tight with tension. In silence, she pulled on her shorts and grabbed her shirt and panties from the couch. She couldn't find her socks and shoes, but she didn't dare stay. In another minute he'd throw her out himself. As it was, the air, thick with anger and betrayal, nearly pushed her out the door.

"I'll stop by later," she said in a low voice. "Maybe we can talk then." She pulled the door shut before Eddie could answer. She wasn't sure he would forgive her this time. And she wasn't sure she would blame him if he didn't.

* * *

Senator Kirk waited on the front porch, rocking in one of the wicker chairs. Ash closed her eyes and pressed her back into the wall. *I can't do this. I can't.* She opened her eyes again. *I have to.* She took a deep breath and stepped outside.

"Dad, what are you doing here?"

"This isn't exactly where I expected to find you." He didn't look at her.

I am not apologizing to him. Her cheeks turned hot. *I am not going to feel guilty about any of this.*

"Your mother called you the other day," he went on.

"Yes."

"Told you we were going to the Vineyard next weekend. As a family."

"And I told her I was working."

At that, her father stood and turned. "Sweetheart, I know why you're here."

You do?

He reached for Ash and pulled her into a hug. "I'm sorry," he whispered into the top of her head. "I'm sorry for everything I put you through."

She began to cry.

"I know what you've gone through the last few months. I know it's been hell."

Her shoulders shook, and the more she tried to stop the tears, the harder they came.

"But please come home. Please. I want to..." He stepped back and swiped a thumb across her cheekbone. "I'm going to make things right. But I need you there. All of you."

Ash hiccupped. "I don't know..."

Her father glanced around, taking in the house with its peeling paint, Eddie's truck parked by the curb, the auto shop logo on her borrowed shirt. "This isn't what you want. Is it? This isn't really you."

How did he know what she wanted? Or who she was? "Maybe it is."

He tilted his chin a little and smiled. "Come on. That—" He nodded toward Eddie's front window. "That's just a distraction. I understand. I know you've been upset about Colin. I won't tell your mother about it. About any of it. Just come back with me."

Something inside Ash shifted. *A distraction? Not Eddie. You don't get to take shots at Eddie. Not when he's the one true thing I've found this summer.* Maybe the one true thing she'd found in her life. "I can't."

"This place has nothing to offer you."

"You don't know that."

Senator Kirk barked out a laugh. "Yes, I do. I've been in a hundred of these towns, sweetheart. They seem charming at first. They're nice to look at. The people are welcoming enough. But there's nothing here for you. Where the hell would you find a job? You're brilliant. You need to live in Boston. Or New York. Not someplace so small. So limiting."

"Limiting?" He would never understand, she thought, and for the first time, she saw the distance in her father's eyes, the cold sliding scale that measured people and places. She was tired of it, tired of wondering where she fell on that scale. And tired of knowing that no one really measured up.

"You should go," she said.

His brows rose. "You're saying no? Just like that?" He paused, rubbing his jaw. "Your mother will be devastated. Colin too."

The mention of her ex was enough. Ash stepped away from her father, toward the door of her home. "I'm sorry you wasted your time coming here. Tell them whatever you want. But I'm not leaving Paradise."

Chapter Twenty

"My father was here." Even as Ash said the words, she couldn't believe them.

"What?" Jen's voice raced up the octave. "In Paradise?"

"Yeah."

"You're kidding."

Ash didn't answer. One hand wound itself through her hair, still damp from the shower.

"You're not kidding?"

"It gets worse."

Jen whistled.

"I was at Eddie's."

"This morning? As in you spent the night there?"

"Yeah."

"Holy shit! It's about time." Jen practically purred her approval across the telephone line. "So how was it?"

"How do you think?" *Amazing. Skin-tingling, heart-turning-inside-out amazing.* Ash almost didn't want to remember, because it made everything worse. Yet as she said it, heat fluttered in her belly. His hands on her skin, his body, lean and hard, his mouth skating across hers and making her ache for more…the memory of it made her dizzy. She lay flat on the hardwood floor of her living room and put a hand over her eyes.

"Ash?"

"I'm here."

"How the hell did your father find you?"

"Who knows?" Connections, an email, a phone call or two. It didn't matter. He might have traced her credit card or gotten a copy of her cell phone bill. He might even have had her followed, from the first day she arrived in town. She sighed. She knew enough of politicians to know they could find out anything they wanted to.

"He wants me to come back to Boston," she said after a minute. "The family's doing a big press thing next weekend. And Mom's really upset that I said no."

"What did you tell him?"

"That I wasn't coming."

"How'd he take that?"

"Not well. Big surprise." She tried to rub away the headache. That wasn't the worst part, though. Not even close. "Eddie's furious."

"Mmm..." Jen clicked her tongue. "Yeah, I guess finding out your new girlfriend is Senator Kirk's daughter might be kind of a rude awakening first thing in the morning."

"No, he's really...he threw me out. I don't know." Ash's voice broke. "I don't think he wants to have anything to do with me."

"He'll get over it."

"I lied to him. About everything."

"Ah, you just didn't tell him the whole truth. There's a difference."

But Ash knew there wasn't, not in Eddie's mind.

"Give him some time. He'll come around."

She closed her eyes against the sun that insisted on poking through the blinds. "What if he doesn't?"

"I'm not answering that." Jen paused. "Why are you so hard on yourself?"

"Because I screwed up."

"Everyone screws up. Don't think you're special because of it. "

"Ouch."

"Aw, honey, you know I'm teasing. Listen, if Mr. Stubborn downstairs doesn't call, or doesn't return your calls, then go down there and knock on his door until he lets you in. Sleep on his doorstep if you have to."

"That sounds a little dramatic."

Jen went on without missing a beat. "Explain why you made up the name, why you didn't tell him who you really were. Come on, anyone else in your situation would have done the same thing."

But neither of her sisters had. Jess and Anne, whatever other faults they might have, had remained in Boston, fielding media questions and carrying on with their lives as Kirk daughters. Only Ashton had turned her back on the family.

"I saw Colin the other day," Jen said.

"So?" Her ex was the absolute last person Ash wanted to think about.

"He looks like hell."

"Good."

"That's what I said. To his face."

"You didn't."

"Sure did. I walked up to him and told him he'd never looked worse in his life, and that it served him right for letting the best thing go that ever happened to him."

"Jen, I love you."

"I know." She laughed. "He agreed with me, too. You know, Callie went back to her old boyfriend. Right after Colin dumped her."

Ash thought about that. In the last few months, everything and everyone in her life had seemed topsy-turvy. Everything she believed so steady had tumbled out of place. But now her father stood guilt-free. Callie and Colin were no more. Next weekend, the Kirk family would travel to Martha's Vineyard, the way they did every summer. Ash remained the only puzzle piece still out of place.

"Jen, I have to go."

"What are you going to do about Eddie?"

"I don't know."

But she did. Ash knew exactly what she needed to do. She needed to go down there and tell him everything, once and for all. She needed to explain why she'd come to Paradise. Why she'd changed her name. Why she'd left Colin, and why she had no intention of taking him back. Sure, she had some things to work out, including one hell of a mess back in Boston, but she needed to start here, with the one man who'd made her feel like no one else ever had.

She needed to start with Eddie.

* * *

Ash stared into her closet. Draped on a hook hung the shirt she'd grabbed from Eddie's apartment that morning. She glanced at the clock. Had it only been a matter of hours since her life had fallen apart? She felt as though she'd been fed through a roller, squeezed of all emotion and energy. She wondered if she turned sideways and looked into the mirror, there'd be nothing left of her but a thin little line.

What did one wear to have the most difficult conversation of one's life? Did she pull on something comfortable, to remind herself that no matter what happened, she'd still be all right? Did she wear something stunning, to make up for the shake in her voice? Or something familiar, to remind the other person that, really, she was the same person as yesterday?

She sighed and reached for her favorite blue tank top, the one with the silver stripe across the front that made her feel a little like a retro Wonder Woman whenever she pulled it on. Not that it mattered. Eddie didn't care what she wore. He never had. It was one of the many reasons she liked him so much.

For the last two hours, his stereo downstairs had blasted raucous, heavy metal music. Some she recognized. Most she didn't. All sounded angry, frenzied, turned up to full volume, as if to block out sound and thought. She pictured him down there, cursing at her and wondering why he'd ever gotten involved in the first place. Ash brushed her hair and pinned some of it back from her face. Much as she wanted to hide behind it, today she needed to look Eddie straight in the eye when she apologized to him. He deserved that much.

The music shut off. Ash stopped in her bedroom doorway, feet searching for her flip-flops. His door opened. Her heart turned over. *Is he coming up here?* Maybe he would save her the shameful walk downstairs, the difficult knock on his door.

But then the front door to the house opened and thudded shut. No, Eddie wasn't coming up here to see her. Eddie was leaving.

Ash hurried through the living room. She pulled back the blinds of the front window and peered into the street in time to see his truck spin in a tight circle and head downtown. Without even stopping at the intersection, he made a hard left, cutting off a minivan. The van honked. Eddie stuck a hand out the window and flipped it off so fast, Ash imagined he meant the middle finger for her as well. Maybe for the whole town of Paradise.

He's going to Frank's. Somehow, she knew that's where he was headed. To work on cars. To forget his frustration. To put in a couple of hours away from the house and away from her.

Something inside Ash squeezed tight, and her chest began to ache. She'd give him his space. "I'm not going to chase him," she whispered. If he left the house, then he didn't want to see her. Not now. Maybe not even today. Jen was right. She would wait.

Even if it just about killed her.

* * *

Three hours passed. Ash did two loads of laundry, cleaned out her refrigerator, and e-mailed both her sisters. Finally, around four-thirty, she fell into a restless sleep on the loveseat.

A dream. Red and blue balloons. Ash on a Ferris wheel, all alone. She looked around, startled, and grabbed at the safety bar. As she spun around and around, the ground grew farther away each time she passed. Someone below her laughed, but when she glanced down, all she could see were faceless people. Flashes of light. Cracks of thunder. She spun in a slow circle, until the next time she looked, the ground had disappeared altogether, and all she could see was the sky falling beneath her.

In a cold sweat, Ash sat straight up and looked around her darkened living room. Rain sliced against her windows; the sky had turned stone gray. The clock read nearly six. Her legs, crunched underneath her, tingled when she tried to move them. She rubbed her eyes and made her way to the front window. *Please let him be home. Please let his truck be there.*

It wasn't.

She straightened her clothes and walked downstairs barefoot. Biting her bottom lip, she knocked on Eddie's door.

Once. No answer.

Twice. Tiny mewed on the other side of the door.

Three times, though she knew by now he wasn't home yet.

I'm going to Frank's. If Eddie's mad at me, fine. But she needed to tell her side of the story. And she needed to do that today, tonight, before they woke up tomorrow with another twelve hours of anger between them.

The drive to the shop took less than five minutes, but still her insides had worked themselves into a giant pretzel by the time she pulled into the lot. The office light burned, and she jumped from her VW. *Please be here.* She peeked around the side of the building, where the employees parked. Five empty spots. And one with a truck inside it, parked at a crooked angle, as if its driver had slammed on the brakes just in time. A red truck. Eddie's truck.

Ash's heart hurled itself into her throat. She had to stop and take a breath before returning to the front door to try the knob. Locked. She frowned and tried again. It didn't budge. Then she read the sign near the bottom of the glass:

Monday-Friday: 9 to 5.
Thursday Nights and Saturday Afternoons: By Appt. Only.

Ash knocked on the glass. She hadn't seen anyone else's vehicle parked outside, but if Eddie was here, wouldn't his boss be as well? She cupped her hands around her eyes and stared inside. It looked as though a dim light illuminated the work area, back behind the office. *Maybe they're hanging out in the shop.* She knocked one more time.

"Ash?" The voice came from behind her.

She spun around, startled. Frank stuck his head out the window of his over-sized diesel truck, which rumbled in place beside her car.

"What are you doing here?"

"I'm..." For a moment, she thought the tears might come again. "I'm looking for Eddie. He's not here?"

The big man cleared his throat. "I—um—no."

"But I saw his truck out back."

Frank nodded, eyes averted. "He was here earlier today, left it parked there." His gaze flicked over her shoulder and back. "He wanted to borrow my bike."

Ash tried to picture Eddie on a ten-speed and couldn't. "Sorry?"

"My Harley. I bought it off a guy last year. Eddie's been messing around with it, wanted to take it for a ride."

"Oh." She shivered and crossed her arms over her chest. "Do you know when he'll be back?"

Frank raised his eyes, but the look of pity inside them almost knocked Ash to the pavement. "Honey, I'm sorry. He met Cass here around three-thirty. The two of 'em have been gone ever since."

Chapter Twenty-One

Cass clutched Eddie around the waist, leaning in close when he took the curve too fast. She shrieked something into his ear, but he couldn't make out the words. Nor did he really want to. When he'd seen her at the convenience store a few hours earlier, she had taken one look at him and known. Black moods and stormy temperaments, Cass could read like an open book. It was the subtleties within a relationship she'd never really gotten. Without saying a word, though, she'd pulled a six-pack of his favorite beer from the cooler and followed him to Frank's. Fifteen minutes later, they were on the bike.

As long as he didn't think too much about it, Eddie was content to ride, as fast as he could. As far as he could. Anything to get away from Paradise. Anything to forget about the woman who had lied her way into his life and then cleaved his heart straight down the middle.

"Cromer's Corners 2 miles" read the sign at the intersection. He slowed for the blinking red light. A right turn took them winding back toward Paradise, a left, nothing but farmland for twenty more miles. Straight ahead lay one of the state's most historic towns, dotted with landmarks, restaurants, and gift shops. With its connection to the Civil War, it remained one of New Hampshire's biggest tourist draws. Eddie gunned the engine and took off again. A few raindrops splattered down his chest and onto his legs.

They could get something to eat and wait out the rain. If he remembered right, there was a local place downtown with fat burgers and endless drafts of beer. That might soothe his anger. Or at least chase it away for a while.

* * *

"Finally." Cass climbed off the bike and strolled into the pub. "God, just in time. I was getting wet." She ran both hands down her chest, smoothing her flimsy tank top over a bra that didn't hide a damn thing. "Nice ride." She looked at him through full lashes.

"Yeah." Eddie found a couple of stools at the end of the bar and pulled them up. "Two tall ones," he told the bartender, opening his wallet.

Cass took her time easing onto the stool beside Eddie, turning the heads of the three other guys at the bar. She wore slim jeans that hugged her hips and slid down just enough in the back to reveal the top of a bright pink thong.

The bartender glanced from her to Eddie and back again. Grunting what Eddie supposed was an approval, he filled two mugs and slid them over. "On the house."

"Bullshit." Eddie tucked a five into the guy's tip jar.

The bartender shrugged. "Suit yourself. But it's ladies' night, two for one."

Eddie didn't respond. He ran a quick hand over his hair. What the hell had happened to him today? How had he managed to wake up next to a woman he thought he was falling for and end up hours later sitting next to his ex-girlfriend?

He didn't want to think about it. He couldn't. The fury of finding out that he'd just opened his soul to someone who was a shadow, a pretend version, a liar, a fake, ate away at his guts. He wanted to puke.

Cass's warm hand crept onto Eddie's knee and stayed there. "How about a shot?" she whispered into his ear. "For old time's sake?"

He shrugged. "Sure." What else did he have to do tonight but get rip-roaring drunk? "Tequila. And two cheeseburgers," he told the bartender. "One with the works. One with ketchup only."

Cass smiled sideways at him. "You remembered." Her hand slid up Eddie's leg. Of course he remembered. He remembered every damn thing. That was the problem.

* * *

Ash lay face down on her bed, listening to Paradise's only jazz station. She should have told Marty she'd take an extra shift. Or she should have stopped down there anyway, had a beer, and listened to J.T.'s stupid jokes. Anything to get out of the house. Anything to keep her mind off what had happened that morning.

Instead she'd eaten cold pizza around seven and crawled into bed. She'd pulled the blinds down tight, not wanting a sliver of light to sneak in and brighten her mood. Now the room pressed down with heavy, unpleasant humidity. She tried to take a breath and tasted stale cotton. Tucking rumpled blankets around her shoulders, she turned to face the wall. The blues rolled over her, thick as murky midnight, and she gave in to tears.

Cass. He went to Cass. She couldn't stop replaying Frank's words and the awful, pitying expression on the man's face. Worse, she couldn't stop thinking about Eddie's ex-girlfriend, with the red hair and the tight clothes and the come-hither look she didn't bother to hide.

He dated her once. It only made sense that he'd go back to her. What guy wouldn't want a woman who looked like that? She drew a forearm across her face and told herself to stop crying.

"...and that was Miles Davis, with his classic rendition of 'Bye Bye Blackbird,'" the DJ said. "To all you lonely lovers out there, this next one's for you..."

Ash looked at the clock. Ten minutes to twelve. She shut off the radio and listened. Nothing but silence from the apartment below. No music patterning the floor with vibrations. No kitten paws racing around the hardwood. No laughter. No voices. Nothing at all.

She fell back against the pillows. "Maybe Dad's right. Maybe Colin's right. Maybe there really is nothing here for me."

What was the point in staying? She supposed part of her had always known that she'd have to go back to Boston. She just didn't think it would be this soon. Well, tomorrow she'd give Marty two weeks' notice. That should give him enough time to find another night manager. By then, the summer would be almost over, and they could sublet her apartment to someone else. If she told Helen she'd be out by mid-August, maybe the landlord could rent to a college student. Ash rolled over and tried to slow her breath, to still her heartbeat, to find a rhythm that would carry her toward sleep. And she tried not to think of all the things she'd miss when she said goodbye.

* * *

"Shit." Eddie stumbled off his barstool and spilled a bowl of peanuts onto the floor.

Cass leaned against him. Her perfume wafted up and reminded him of other days, earlier days, when he'd breathed in that scent and wanted more, always more, of it. "You can't drive home."

"No kidding." Double-shit. He hadn't meant to get so slobbering drunk. He'd just wanted a few shots, some beers to chase them down, something to mellow him out so he could forget Ashley Kirtland. Or Ashton Kirk. Or whatever the hell her name really was.

"There's a motel next block over," offered the bartender. "I can call you a cab."

Cass wound her arm through Eddie's and tugged him toward the door. "The motel'll be fine," she said over her shoulder. "We can walk."

Outside, the air felt good as Eddie drew it into his lungs. Fresh. Clean. Forgiving. Everything he wasn't. The rain had stopped, though puddles still dotted the pavement. He lifted the two helmets off the back of Frank's bike.

"I gotta text Frank, tell him I'll get the Harley back tomorrow."

Cass pressed her hand against his. "You already did. About an hour ago."

"Really?" Eddie rubbed his forehead and tried to remember. He pulled out his cell phone and checked. "Oh. Yeah."

"There's the motel." Cass pointed across the street.

A few hundred yards away, Eddie could make out the blur of a neon sign. "Vacancy," he read. "We'll get two rooms."

The redhead put one hand on a hip. "Like hell we will." She snuggled herself under his arm. "You need some comforting, Eddie West. I don't know who broke your heart, or how she did it, but tonight you need some grade-A ex-girlfriend lovin', and that's exactly what I'm gonna give you." She slipped a hand inside his back pocket.

Eddie didn't answer, just started to walk. What he really needed was a soft bed and about a thousand hours of sleep. Then, in the morning, he'd let some greasy home fries ease his hangover while he went about shoveling the pieces of his heart under the carpet. He glanced over. But hey, if a woman like Cassandra Perkins wanted to keep herself warm beside him in the meantime, he wasn't sure he had any objections.

Not tonight, anyway.

Chapter Twenty-Two

Consciousness came slowly, working its way into Ash's bedroom on leaden feet.

I'm still in Paradise, she thought after a minute of staring at the ceiling. *For now, anyway.* A blink at the clock and a long swig of water reminded her of last night's decision. She'd give Blues and Booze two more weeks. But no more.

She swung her feet over the edge of the bed. Though nearly nine, no light came through her blinds. She padded across the room and peered outside. Rain spit against her windows, not heavy, just steady.

"Great. Another stupid, gray day." Just what she needed to match her mood. Ash headed for the bathroom, glad she'd taken a lunch shift to fill up the empty afternoon. *I'll tell Marty when I get there.* She eased her way under the shower's hot spray. No reason to call him earlier. He'd throw enough of a fit as it was.

She felt more than a little guilty about leaving Blues and Booze, especially since she'd been running the place a couple nights a week, but what was she supposed to do?

This place has nothing to offer you...

"Dad's right," she said aloud. The sooner she went back to Boston and faced down her demons, the better. She had a degree from one of the top law schools in the country. She knew of a half-dozen firms in the city who'd give their eyeteeth to hire a Harvard grad, especially one with the last name Kirk. She'd have no problem working herself back into that way of life. And if her father and her family needed her, then it was about time she stopped acting like a spoiled child with her heart broken. She was twenty-six, not sixteen. She needed to get it together and go to Martha's Vineyard. *What's the worst that can happen?*

Ash turned off the shower in time to hear her phone ring.

Eddie. The thought that it might be him shot adrenaline straight into her soul. *He's calling to talk. He wants to make up.* It wasn't too late after all. She wrapped a towel around her head and grabbed her robe. All thoughts of Boston and her father and the Vineyard fled. Still wet, she skated into the living room.

But her voicemail picked up before she could answer, and as soon as hope had lifted inside her heart, it was gone again. She pressed the button to listen to the message, but one look at the screen told her who had called.

"Ash? Marty here."

She sank onto the loveseat and rested her head on one palm. Of course it wasn't Eddie. Look what she'd done by lying to him. Look at everything she'd ruined.

"Got something to ask you." Marty hacked up phlegm for a few seconds before continuing. "And, ah, I know you're coming in to work lunch today, but I've got a meeting down in the city."

The city? As in Boston? Marty rarely left Paradise, as far as Ash knew, though he'd been gone a lot of nights this summer. What was the guy up to? Got a woman? She couldn't imagine it. Gambling addiction?

"...so could you give me a call when you can?"

Ash erased the message. She might as well get it over with. He probably wanted her to cover as manager tonight, or maybe pull a double tomorrow. She'd call and find out for sure and tell him about her leaving at the same time. He wouldn't like it, but—

Marty picked up on the first ring. "Ash?"

"Hi. Got your message."

"Ah, hey there." He coughed.

"Oughta get those lungs looked at," she said almost without thinking. She knew he wouldn't listen; she told him the same thing two or three times a week. It wasn't like you could change the habits of a chronic smoker. The things people carried around for a lifetime worked their claws inside the skin and stayed there.

"So what's up?"

"Ash, listen. I'm gonna need someone up here full-time to run the restaurant. I'm thinking about opening another place down near Salem. Cater to the college crowd."

"What are you talking about?"

"I've been talking to a buddy of mine these last few weeks. He's got the dough, likes my ideas. Wants to go in partners with me."

"Really?" Ash's brows rose. She couldn't picture Marty leaving Paradise, let alone opening another version of Blues and Booze. But then again, she'd never really looked past his yellow teeth and bloodshot eyes. Maybe the restaurant business had grown on him. Maybe, after all this time, he did want more. Maybe he wanted expansion, a place that drew a younger, bigger crowd. More money. More possibilities. "So wait, you're leaving town?"

"For a while, if I can find someone to take care of the place here. I'll be spending most of my time down there, next few months, anyway. So, ah, if you're interested, like to offer you the manager job. Full-time." He chuckled, wheezing only a little. "Well, probably be more than full-time, 'cause you know what the hours are like. You can hire someone to work under you, if you want. Part-time, cover the nights."

"Marty, I can't—"

"Don't say no right away," he interrupted. "I know it probably ain't the dream job you got lined up inside your head. But you're damn good at it. The customers like you. Lot of 'em come in to see you. But you don't take any crap from anyone either, and that's good." He paused to draw a rattly breath. "I ain't never considered opening another place 'til this opportunity came along. And you... you're okay. You got the hang of it. And you're about the only person with enough brains to keep it going. So if you want to stay in town for a while, give it a shot, I'd appreciate it. Really."

Ash didn't say anything. *Stay in Paradise? Run Blues and Booze?* It was ridiculous. She couldn't. She'd do a terrible job. Besides, she'd make what? A few thousand dollars? Barely enough to cover the rent in this second-floor apartment. No way. It made no sense.

Then why didn't she just tell Marty thanks, but no thanks? Why didn't she tell him she'd be gone in two weeks, back in Boston where she belonged? Why, instead, did she tell him she'd think about it?

Because, she decided as she threw on an old pair of shorts and a halter top and stepped into the rain, she had finally, and completely, lost her mind.

* * *

The rain let up shortly after Ash rounded the corner of Lycian Street, and by the time she headed downtown, past the church green, all that remained was a fuzzy sky with some sun poking through. She bent her head against the wind, shoulders hunched, and walked past the restaurant. Past the tiny yellow-sided library, where Celia Darling waved a hand as she gathered books from the return bin. Past Annie's Fabrics and the Used Book Depot, sharing space in a corner building. At the convenience store she turned, giving a nod to the guy who stood in the doorway. Harry Broker. Came in sometimes with his teenage daughter, weekends when she visited from her mom's.

Ash shook her head. She couldn't keep thinking about the people she knew, the connections she'd made here in Paradise. It had been just a summer detour, a distraction, as her father had put it. A few weeks of getting to know the locals didn't mean she belonged here, even if Marty had just offered her the perfect opportunity for staying. She dodged a baseball that rolled into the street and kept her eyes down. She didn't want to see who it belonged to or play the matching game with another local face.

Another turn, this time onto a quiet street, thick with oak trees. St. James Avenue curved up toward the community college, and she followed it, slowing as the hill grew steeper. Here the houses pushed together, one atop the next like postage stamps in a line. All one-level, all neatly tended, almost all brick with white or black trim and flowers on the stoop. Here and there, a flag in the window or a bronze nameplate broke the pattern. *Don't they mind? Don't they want to look distinct? Or is there comfort in fitting in?*

Ahead of her, a wrought iron gate stood open beside a sign welcoming her to New Hampshire Central Junior College. Ash wrapped her fingers around the bars and stared at the squat buildings, made of the same red brick as the houses behind her. Near the entrance stood a white building with cupolas on top and a sign that read "Admissions" in front. In the background she could see the three story library accented with flowerbeds and a stone lion statue sitting regally in front. It looked like every other local school, plopped in a tiny town, anywhere in the country.

Except it wasn't. This one belonged to Paradise, New Hampshire. And suddenly, she heard Eddie's voice again inside her head.

"... people have the same problems no matter where you go. Big city or small town, people get hurt. Friends steal from each other. Men cheat on their wives. Kids sneak out at night and get drunk while their parents think they're sleeping. People get divorced, same as every other place...At least here, in Paradise, you know someone's got your back. You know there's always someone you can count on, someone you grew up with who's gonna forgive you no matter how bad you screw things up..."

She turned away from the college. Two benches flanked the fence, and she dropped onto one, not caring that rainwater had puddled inside it.

Is that why she liked it? Because there was something here that made her feel like she belonged? Something that told her people would look out for her? Stand up for her? Forgive her when she screwed things up?

She ran one finger along the bench's scrollwork.

"...I know it probably ain't the dream job you got lined up inside your head. But you're damn good at it. The customers like you. Lot of 'em come in to see you..."

True, the town didn't seem to care who she was. The people living here hadn't asked questions when she'd moved in. They'd taken her word and welcomed her just the same. And she liked that she hadn't relied on her last name to find a job. To make connections. To make love.

Eddie chose me. Not my pedigree. Not my degree. He chose his screwed-up, neurotic, upstairs neighbor who slept late and occasionally spilled coffee on people and chewed her thumbnail when she got nervous. *He chose me.* The realization washed over her in hot waves.

She had to tell him how he'd changed her, how this place had changed her. If Marty was offering her a chance to stay, to explore the possibilities that Paradise held for her, then Ash wasn't about to say no. Not just yet. Not when everything between her and Eddie felt so unfinished.

She stood and made her way back down St. James. At the bottom, she broke into a jog. The church clock boomed out eleven o'clock, and she hurried on. Why was it that time only dragged when you wanted to rush it along, and when you really wanted to slow it, it insisted on running away from you?

She headed back to Lycian Street. If Eddie wasn't home yet, she'd leave him a note. She'd wedge it inside his door and ask him to come to Blues and Booze later on. She didn't care that maybe he'd spent the night with Cass. She had explaining to do. And apologies to make.

"Hi, Ash!" Toby Darling, Celia's son, sat on the front step of the library, tossing a baseball from one hand to the other.

A few weeks back, she'd given the ten-year-old a dish of leftover ice cream, the night the power went out and every restaurant on Main Street had to empty their freezers. He'd adored her ever since.

"Hi yourself," she answered, waving back. The sun winked in and out of clouds, and she felt it press down on the back of her neck. Warm. Comforting. Like a hand urging her home.

She practically skipped the last block, rehearsing her speech to Marty in between thinking of the first thing she wanted to tell Eddie. Not to mention the first thing she wanted to do to him. With him. Her face burned a little, but she didn't care. When you figured out what it was you wanted, you'd do whatever it took to get it back. Even if that meant staring down the vixen from your lover's past.

Ash cracked her knuckles as anxiety welled up inside her. Due at work in less than an hour, she didn't have a lot of time. Her fingers dug inside her pocket as she rounded the corner, and because her house keys got stuck in a loose thread, she was looking down as she made her way to the porch steps.

So he saw her first. He spoke first. And when she raised her head to see who waited for her with a smile in his voice, all breath left her body. Tall and impossibly good-looking, the kind of good-looking that belonged on a magazine cover, Colin Parker stood on the porch of number two Lycian Street. He winked. Cocked his head to one side, the way she remembered too well. Grinned that camera-ready smile that flipped her stomach over and loped down the steps to meet her. All Ash could do was stand there and stare as his rolling bass voice carried her back through time.

"Hi, babe. God, it's good to see you again."

Chapter Twenty-Three

Garbled country music jarred Eddie awake. "Shit." He reached a hand in the direction of the motel nightstand and jabbed his thumb at the alarm clock. There. Silence. Falling back against the flat pillow, he flung an arm over his face. Jesus, but he had a headache to beat all headaches. And he guessed he'd forgotten to close the curtains last night, because now a strip of sunlight streamed across the bed, eye-level.

"Eddie?"

He squirmed. For a few minutes, he'd forgotten he wasn't alone in the bed.

Cass poked a finger at his bare shoulder. "You feeling okay?"

He didn't answer. What the hell did she think? The last twenty-four hours had tossed him into the center of a tornado. If he looked in the mirror, he wasn't even sure whose face he'd see, or if he'd recognize it. Couple that with the fact that last night's binge had left him with someone playing drums inside his skull and someone else painting the roof of his mouth with acid, and no, he wasn't feeling okay. Or anything close to it.

She trailed her fingertips along his spine. "Want some water?"

He shook his head, still staring at the backs of his eyelids.

Did I sleep with her? He didn't want to ask, didn't want to know. The bed dipped, squeaking a little as she got up.

"I'm going for some coffee," she said. "I'll bring you back some."

Eddie heard the soft slipping of fabric over skin as she dressed. Grunting, he waited until the door closed before he turned over and opened his eyes. He took his time surveying the room, looking for signs of a knockdown, drag-out, all-clothes-off-in-sixty-seconds adventure the minute they'd stepped inside the room last night.

It's happened before. I'd be a fool to think it couldn't have happened again.

But he didn't see much out of place. No chairs tipped onto the carpet. No ice spilled the length of the dresser. Even the bedspread covering his lower half, in some God-awful plum pattern, appeared smooth and tucked in. Only his shorts and shirt lay tossed on the floor, alongside the two motorcycle helmets.

Eddie slid from the bed and lurched into the bathroom. He dropped the toilet lid and slipped to an awkward seat. Leaning forward, he rested his head in both hands and stared at his lap. At least he still wore his boxers. That was a good sign. He couldn't remember actually doing anything with Cass by the time they'd collapsed inside this wreck of a room, but then again, he couldn't remember walking the two blocks from the bar to the motel, either, or checking in at the front desk.

"Idiot," he said to his feet. He turned on the cold water. The fact that Ashton Kirk had just twisted him inside out didn't give him any excuse to ride around New Hampshire, screwing the first willing woman who came along. *Pull yourself together, West. Other women have treated you worse than Ash did.* Didn't mean he had to crawl into a hole and wait for next year. *Jesus, she's just a woman. Thousands more in the damn sea, remember?*

He stood, grabbed a towel, and wet it until it dripped. Then he slapped it across his cheeks and draped it around the back of his neck. He spat into the toilet and flushed. The way he figured it, he had two choices. One, he could head back to Paradise, ignore her for the rest of the summer, and by the time autumn rolled around, be back to his usual self. Or two, he could go back to Lycian Street, march upstairs, and tell her exactly what he thought of the lies she'd told.

Eddie ground his teeth together. He didn't really like either option, because both required him to turn his back on the first woman who'd made him feel alive in years. Still, what choice did he have? He jammed the heel of one hand against his forehead and tried to ignore the heave working its way up his throat. *Gonna be sick,* he thought, a second before last night's burgers and tequila caught up with him. Bending over the toilet just in time, he hugged the cold porcelain with both arms as he sank to his knees and lost everything inside him.

* * *

"Eddie?" It was Cass's voice. He wasn't sure how much time had passed. Only a few minutes, probably. Struggling to a stand, he flushed the toilet and rubbed a hand over his face.

"Yeah." He pushed his way back into the dingy bedroom. Cass waited by the bed, sipping a steaming cup of coffee. Another sat on the dresser.

She cocked her head, hair streaming over one shoulder. "Gonna be all right?"

He shrugged, reached for his clothes and pulled them on. "Thanks for the joe." He took a long gulp, letting it burn his lips. Black. Good.

"You're welcome." She ran a finger down the side of his face. "You look like hell."

"Tell me something I don't know."

She smiled and sank to a seat in one of the chairs near the window. "Okay." She paused. "We didn't sleep together last night."

Eddie jerked a little at her words. "You're...well, I..."

She laughed outright then. "Oh, please. I know you've been wondering since the minute you woke up. I know you, Eddie. I know that guilty look that makes your eyes all squinty."

He felt himself redden and stared down at the coffee, as if it might hold the answers within its darkness. "Listen, I'm sorry," he said after a minute. "I didn't mean to drag you all the way over here just to listen to my problems."

She flipped a hand into the air. "I didn't do much listening. After you fell asleep halfway in the door, it was all I could do to get you undressed..." Her eyelashes fluttered toward her lap, coquettish. "Thought I might get a little action after all."

A smile tugged at his face.

Cass shrugged. "But you kept talking about Ashton this, and Ashton that." She looked back up at him. "I thought her name was Ashley."

So did I.

Eddie found his wallet, tossed in the open drawer of the nightstand, and stuffed it into his back pocket. "I gotta get back home. Things to take care of. You ready?"

She shook her head. "I have a couple friends in town. Called 'em this morning." She spun the watch on her thin wrist. "We're meeting over at the diner in twenty minutes. I figured you could use some time to yourself."

He nodded, relieved. The ride back to Paradise, the sorting out he needed to do, was better suited for solitude. He bent down and planted a kiss on his ex-girlfriend's cheek. "You're okay," he mumbled. "Thanks."

Cass leaned back in the chair, letting her glance slide down his torso. "No problem. Make sure she knows what she's missing."

Eddie smiled for real this time and dropped a hand onto her shoulder. Then he picked up the motorcycle helmets and headed out into the sun.

* * *

He took the long way back to Paradise. Avoiding the main road, he chose the back ones instead, the narrow ones that wound their way through woods and past lakes and by the occasional house or gas station. He drove slowly at first, savoring the feel of the handlebars and the hum of the engine beneath him. He waved to a little girl playing in her front yard and a pair of joggers. He watched fields and trees change places every mile or so.

But try as he might, Eddie couldn't get her out of his head. Ash. Ashton Kirk. Okay, the damn senator's daughter. That's who she was, then. His grip tightened. And wrong or right, somewhere in between all the stories they'd told each other that summer, he'd fallen in love with her. He ground to a halt as a stop sign caught him by surprise.

In love with her? Are you out of your mind? He shook his head at the inner voice that argued back. Bottom line, that's what it came down to. Sure, Ash had lied to him, and that broke something inside him. It made him ache, the idea that he'd bared his soul while she'd kept hers banded tightly up. It made him wonder how she really felt about him, and what else she might be hiding.

What it didn't do, though, was change the way Eddie felt when he was with her. It didn't change the fact that in meeting Ash, in living with her, in spending all those minutes together that added up to something more, he'd come alive for the first time in three years.

She'd taken away his guard. She'd made him laugh. She'd pissed him off. She'd made him remember what it was like to be a regular guy, someone who wasn't trying to get into bed with a woman because it was easier than talking to her. *God, she reminded me I still had a heart beating under the mess I became after the accident.*

Eddie sped up as he reached Paradise's town limits. The

thoughts tumbled faster and faster inside his head. He needed to get back to Lycian Street. He needed to see her. He needed to talk to her.

Whoever she really is.

Chapter Twenty-Four

"Don't touch me." Before Colin could take her by both arms and pull her in for a kiss, Ash twisted away from him.

He stopped, and his smile froze. "I just—okay. I'm sorry."

She stuck her hands into her pockets, house keys digging into one palm. First her father. Now her ex-boyfriend. Ash let out a long breath. Her legs grew unsteady, and she refused to look at him again. She couldn't take any more surprise visitors. She was about torn in half as it was.

"What are you doing here?"

"That's a nice way to say hello."

"I told you I wasn't coming home. And I didn't tell you where I lived. Which means you took it upon yourself to find me when I didn't want to be found." She looked at the peeling paint beside him, the rusted door hinges, the weeds growing alongside the geraniums in the yard.

He exhaled. "Thought maybe you'd reconsidered."

"Why would you think that?"

Colin's chin jerked in the direction of the house. "This is where you decided to spend your summer?"

"What's wrong with it?"

He swiped a hand over his close cut, dark blonde hair. "Nothing, babe. I just..."

"My father told you where I was. Didn't he?"

Colin raised both palms to the sky. "Guilty. But only because I called him and told him I needed to see you. Needed to make up for the stupidest thing I'd ever done."

Suddenly, the fire left Ash's heart, and she sank into the chair farthest away from him. She didn't have the energy for this. "Whatever. Stay, leave, I don't care. I'm not going back to Boston. I already told him that. I don't care if he sent you to try and convince me."

"He didn't."

She doubted that, but she kept her mouth shut.

Colin sat in the chair across from her and folded his fingers together. "Okay, I get that you were mad. That you needed space."

"That's an understatement." She tried not to look directly at him, because she had a feeling that if she did, he'd burn her to the core. Colin Parker was—always had been—a too-bright sun shining down on Ash. He pulled her close. He drew her into his orbit.

"I wanted to apologize. In person." Eyes on the ground, he cleared his throat. "I was a total ass. Really. That thing with Callie—"

"I don't want to talk about it."

"It was a complete mistake. I was juvenile. Idiotic." Another throat-clearing. "And yeah, the thing that happened with your dad, it shook me up some."

Ash rubbed the back of her neck, trying to loosen the muscles there. "Well, me too." *I wasn't exactly a saint when it came to defending him. I guess we both ran away from it in our own ways.*

Colin reached for her hand, brushed his fingers across the back of it for an instant. "We were good together, right? I want to try again."

Oh, God. The words she'd wanted to hear three months ago. Even two months ago. Ash's skin burned from where he'd touched it. "I don't think—"

"Hear me out. Please." He inched his chair closer, so that their knees touched. Skin to skin, breath meeting breath. Ash's heart sped up. "We're a good match," he went on. He caught her gaze and held it with those dark eyes. "We're headed the same way. We want the same things."

Oh, really?

"We'd be good for each other." He wound his fingers through hers. "Or you'd be good for me, anyway." He grinned. "But I'd try, babe. I'd try to be the best goddamned husband you could ever wish for."

Ash drew her hand away. "What are you talking about?"

Colin rose, towering over her for a moment before he folded himself into a crouch at her feet. The boards creaked beneath him, and for an instant, she thought of the night she and Eddie had stood there, after a dinner shift. After the first time they fought. Before the first time they kissed.

"Thanks for walking me home."

"No problem."

"See you tomorrow, I guess."

"See ya."

Colin spoke again, interrupting the memory.

"Ashton." He reached into his front pocket and pulled out a small black box.

She drew in her breath and held it. That box didn't contain what she thought it did. It couldn't. The wind picked up and crickets scratched their legs together. The flowers near the sidewalk swayed. Beyond the hills, thunder rumbled.

"It's going to rain," she said. "We should go inside."

Thunder announced itself again, closer this time. As if it hovered in the hills behind the college, or came up from the ground beneath her. Or turned the corner on two wheels.

In slow motion Ash looked past him, just as the motorcycle veered onto Lycian Street. Just as its rider slowed to a stop in front of the house. Just as he pulled off his helmet and looked at her and Colin. *Oh, Eddie.* His eyes, wide at first with something like hope, dimmed as his gaze moved across them. Even from a distance Ash saw his face redden. Something clutched inside her chest.

It's my heart tearing in two. Stretching in opposite directions. Breaking apart.

Colin took her hand, forcing her attention back to where he still knelt in front of her. "Ash, I love you." The last word cracked. "I want to spend my life with you." He flipped open the box, and an enormous diamond ring flashed up at her. Emerald cut, the way she'd once told him she'd wanted. Close to two carats, if she had to guess. And more diamonds set along the delicate band of platinum. Sunlight caught a rainbow of color as his hand shook a little.

"Marry me, babe. Please. Make me the happiest guy in the world."

* * *

Eddie pulled up behind a sleek silver BMW. Who the hell did that belong to? For a minute he wondered if Ash's father had stayed in town. Then his gaze traveled up to the front porch. Eddie straddled the bike and stared. The whole way back to Paradise, he'd thought it over, and here was the thing: he wanted to work things out with Ash. He wanted to see if they could push aside the mess and make a go of it. Just the two of them. He thought maybe they could. He thought maybe they had a chance.

But now...

She wasn't alone. The realization stopped him before he got off the bike. She was with another guy. After twenty-four hours?

Ash glanced over and saw Eddie at that moment, and her eyes widened. A messy ponytail fell down her back, and her top looked damp. He wondered if she'd been up half the night, or out walking since dawn. Her face flushed, and her hands worked themselves in and out of her pockets. She bit her bottom lip and turned away again.

What the hell was going on? With his head still throbbing enough to remind him of last night's mistake, Eddie rubbed a hand across his eyes. He didn't recognize the guy kneeling on the porch, in his light blue shirt and ironed shorts and woven leather sandals. But he held something in his hand that Ash kept staring at. Eddie took a few steps up the sidewalk.

"Colin, I don't..." As the guy stood, close to six three or four if Eddie had to guess, Ash put a hand on his chest. Her words fell away, but she didn't stop looking at him.

That's Colin? The ex-boyfriend? Eddie's earlier cup of coffee burned in the center of his chest. As he watched, Colin slipped a ring onto Ash's finger, wrapped an arm around her waist, and pulled her in for a kiss. One hand swept the hair off her forehead. The other pressed five fingers into the small of her back. Possessive. Wanting. He hadn't even looked Eddie's way.

Eddie's head jerked back as if someone had caught him square across the jaw. He felt sick, almost feverish. Stumbling, he backed toward the bike. *Mistake*...the word echoed inside his head. *A total mistake, to come back here.* To think she'd want to be with him. To think she wouldn't go back to her other life the minute she had the chance. Thunder growled, and a few drops of rain pattered the back of his neck.

"Eddie, wait!"

He didn't turn around. One leg over the motorcycle, and it revved to life. The rain picked up; the wind swept in and chilled him bone deep. He couldn't have cared less. Barreling through the stop sign, he headed downtown. He wove around a stupid Civic going thirty miles an hour and an equally stupid mini-van with a bumper sticker that read "I Brake for Manatees."

Manatees? Where do you live, lady, fucking Florida? Look around. Only small-town USA up here in New Hampshire. No ocean. No big cities. No place anyone would want to stay and build a life, that's for sure. Under his breath came every curse word he could think of, most of them directed at Ash. A few at himself. What an idiot he'd been to fall for her, someone he'd known less than three months.

On he rode, faster at every chance, savoring the silence, the speed, the rush of air that stilled his thoughts after awhile. *Gotta get myself a bike. Or talk Frank into letting me buy this one.* The rain came down harder with every mile, and he welcomed it. Only when he reached the hairpin curve that headed out of town did Eddie realize he'd left his helmet sitting on the curb back on Lycian Street.

Chapter Twenty-Five

Ash stumbled down the porch steps as Eddie jumped back onto the motorcycle. He sped through the intersection and left a strip of burnt rubber three feet long. Colin's hand fell onto her shoulder, but she shook it off.

"Colin..." She looked down at the ring on her finger. Already it felt heavy with the weight of the gem, not to mention his offer and the promise it held if she said yes. "I can't make this decision."

His Adam's apple moved once, in a hard swallow that betrayed his disappointment. "It's okay. Take some time. Take as much as you need."

He didn't look mad, or impatient, or as though he wanted to change his mind. He just looked sad, as if he knew maybe he'd waited too long. As if he understood he'd made the wrong decision and now couldn't right it.

"I know...ah...that maybe you didn't expect it," he went on.

"You think?"

Colin reddened. "Took me a while to figure things out." He stared at his feet. "I screwed up. But I don't want to lose you. I'll do whatever it takes."

Ash sank onto the bottom step. She didn't want to blame Colin for her heartache. She didn't want the exhaustion of hating him anymore. She wanted to watch the rain fall and not count all the times she'd walked with him in it. She wanted to sleep for more than two nights in a row without waking up thinking of him. She wanted what he was offering her: the chance to forgive, move on, and change the past.

But that made it harder. She wished he wouldn't be so damn nice about it. *Give me an ultimatum, and I'll throw the ring across the porch and tell you to go to hell. But don't tell me you'll wait. Don't turn into this sensitive guy I don't even know.*

"You broke my heart." She meant to hurt him with the words, to make him feel one ounce of the pain he'd put her through. "You can't just make everything better with an apology and a ring."

Colin nodded. "I know." He looked down at his hands. "I don't blame you if you tell me to go to hell," he added. "I guess I probably deserve it."

"You do." But her voice faltered.

He bent and brushed a kiss across her cheek. "I still love you," he said again. "And I'll wait, however long it takes, for you to see that I'm serious. That I want us to work." He stopped halfway down the sidewalk, shoulders hunched against the rain. "I've got a room at the Holiday Inn over by the interstate. I'll be there until tomorrow." He paused. "Then I'm heading home. Be at the Vineyard with your folks next weekend, if you want. Or if not, then... just call me, okay? Let me know."

She blinked, surprised, at the kindness in his words. The sincerity. Maybe he really was sorry. She glanced down at her left hand. Maybe it wasn't too late for a life like that.

"I'll call you," she said.

He nodded and jogged to his car, slipping inside and turning the wipers on high. The next moment the BMW turned the corner, a silver streak in the distance. *He's gone, just like Eddie.* Only Colin was willing to wait for her. Eddie wouldn't even stop to let her explain. She shivered in the damp air.

After a minute—or ten, she wasn't quite sure—Ash let herself into the house. Halfway upstairs she had to stop and catch her breath. Palms wet with perspiration, she tugged on the ring until it slipped from her finger. She held it up to the light.

Gorgeous. And perfect, of course. She wouldn't expect less from Colin Parker. But what did it mean? That he still loved her? That he was sorry? That he wanted her back, along with her name, her future, and the benefits they offered him? If she sliced away his top layer, could she see through to the bottom? Was there anything in the middle? Anything past the good looks and the intelligence that made him a shoe-in for political office?

Ash shoved the ring into her front pocket and made her way up the final few steps.

But if she did the same thing to Eddie, what would she see there? A man too angry to trust anyone again? Someone who was happy spending his whole life bouncing in and out of beds in Paradise? Or someone who could see through the layers she wrapped around herself?

She reached for her cell phone and punched in the number for the restaurant. Sometime while Colin was on his knee and Eddie was staring across the lawn, she'd heard the church bell ring twelve times, which meant she was now officially late for work.

"...I'll be there in ten minutes," she promised J.T. She walked to the front window and studied the sky, blue-black and scorched with lightning. She'd have to take her car. She couldn't walk in this.

She'd bring an extra shirt, just in case she got soaked running across the parking lot. Maybe an extra pair of socks. Cataloging the things she needed to take care of in the next five minutes helped Ash keep her mind off the bigger things she had to figure out in the next twenty-four hours. *Get from here to the bedroom. Then from the bedroom to the car. Then from the car to the restaurant.* She could deal with the rest later.

Ash glanced outside. Near the curb, Eddie's motorcycle helmet lay in the rain. She started, as if the lightning outside had reached into the apartment and sizzled her. Eddie's helmet. Here. On the ground. Not on his head. Not protecting him. Without stopping to put on her shoes, she ran out into the rain and retrieved it, laying it in front of his door.

She hated motorcycles, had lost a classmate back in high school to a violent accident. Something stole the heat from her face as she stumbled upstairs. She couldn't think about Evan Traler's funeral, or the fact that his parents had a closed casket because his face peeled off when he hit the pavement going eighty miles per hour without a helmet.

Without a helmet...

Ash shook her head as she made her way to the car and negotiated the water filling Main Street. Eddie had seen enough damage from careless driving to know better. He'd be careful. Right? But that look on his face when he spun away from the sidewalk. That anger.

Stop it. He'll be fine. His brother had died in a car accident, for God's sake. He wouldn't risk putting his parents through that again. She pulled into the lot behind the restaurant. That thought felt right. That thought, she could believe and find comfort in.

When she got home from her shift, she'd go see him. Maybe they could talk rationally. Maybe she could convince him that whatever he'd seen on the porch wasn't the whole truth. Maybe, with tiny steps, they could sift through their feelings and the lies that she'd told. Maybe, just looking up at him, feeling his hands on hers again, would help her make a decision.

Baby steps. Just get yourself through the next few hours. You'll be fine. He'll be fine.

She skipped over a puddle, not knowing that this time, she was wrong.

* * *

Near the end of the lunch shift, the crowd at Blues and Booze finally trickled to a stop. With a single family in a booth and a couple of guys at the bar, the two waitresses headed into the kitchen. Ash leaned against the stainless steel counter, exhausted and starving. She grabbed a packet of soup crackers and realized she hadn't eaten a thing since breakfast. Since before she'd gotten the phone call from Marty. Since before she'd walked her way through town only to return home and find Colin waiting for her, with an engagement ring and a promise of forever. Crackers fell from her hand and made a yellow crumb pile on the counter. Without the distraction of taking orders and running food, the memories returned, painfully sharp. Had all that happened just today? It seemed as though a thousand hours had passed since she woke up.

"Everything okay?" Lacey began refilling ketchup bottles.

"Fine."

"I heard Marty asked you to take over full-time."

Ash didn't answer. News traveled fast. Too fast, sometimes.

"So are you thinking about it?"

"I don't know. I never really planned on staying in town." She grabbed a pile of napkins, fresh from the dry cleaner. "I only sublet my apartment for the summer." Edge to edge, fold once and then twice. Her fingers followed the rhythm that had become second nature that summer.

Lacey chuckled. "Yeah. Funny how plans change, huh?"

Ash finished folding and carried an armful of napkins to the closet. On her way back, she took a detour to the ladies' room. She didn't feel like making conversation, even with Lacey. How was she supposed to answer Marty's question with Colin's hanging over her? Sinking onto the toilet seat, she sighed and rubbed her legs. The ring, still in her pocket, dug into her thigh. She pulled it out. Look at it fifty different ways, think about all the things it meant she had to choose, it still was the most beautiful piece of jewelry she'd ever seen.

"Marry me...make me the happiest guy in the world..."

The door banged open, and a pair of feet appeared in the stall beside her. "Ash? J.T. said Marty called, wants us to close up early today."

"Why?" She glanced at her watch. Almost four. She wasn't ready to go home. She wasn't ready to see Eddie, to call Colin, to make any kind of decision. She wanted to wait until the wee hours, tomorrow's dawn maybe. Not mid-afternoon of a gray, lifeless day. She flushed and headed for the sinks, avoiding her reflection in the mirror.

"Guess the storm's pretty bad," Lacey said. "Shoot. I could have used the dinner shift. Lunch tips weren't so good."

Ash lathered up and watched the soap swirl into the drain. *I wish I could do that. I wish I could just vanish in a whirlpool until I sort out my life.* Hide in a dark hole until things on the outside made sense again. She frowned. Except she'd come to Paradise with the intention of doing just that, and look where it had gotten her. Her shoulders hunched up. Maybe you couldn't ever run away from your life. Maybe the big choices did follow you no matter where you went.

Back in the bar, J.T. nodded over his toothpick when she asked about the weather.

"Yep. Marty said the bridge to Forestburg's under water. He's stuck down in Salem overnight. Plus the news said there are a couple of accidents on the other side of town. He said to forget it, go on home."

Outside, lightning sliced the street into jagged white pieces, and the rain poured down, heavier than ever. Ash nodded. If she were calling the shots, she'd say the same thing. No use staying open. The way this weather looked, she couldn't imagine anyone in Paradise leaving the comfort of their couches.

The telephone rang.

"Blues and Booze," J.T. answered. "We're getting ready to close... oh, yeah. Hang on a minute." He held out the receiver. "For you."

Ash frowned. No one called her at work. "Who is it?"

"Dunno. Some guy."

"That's helpful."

J.T. shrugged and started counting his drawer

"Ashton Kirk?" She didn't recognize the voice.

"Yes?"

The man paused, giving way to a cough. But when he spoke again, she knew who it was. She knew before he told her his name. She knew from the way he formed his vowels. She knew from the way he dropped the end of his sentences, from the way he stopped every so often when the words became too hard to say. She knew because he spoke exactly the same way his son did.

"Eddie's been in an accident. He's asking for you."

Chapter Twenty-Six

A face. Blurred and dark. Eddie tried to sit up. "Whoa." Hands on his shoulders pushed him back. "Take it easy."

He tried to ask where he was, and why the hell the lights above him were so bright, but when he opened his mouth, nothing came out. He tried again. A mumble this time. In fragmented pieces, the room took shape around him. White everywhere. Shadows he couldn't make out. Noises he didn't recognize: humming and beeping and mechanical burping. Something wrapped tight around his arm. And a God-awful smell. Seconds later, he placed it.

Oh, Jesus Christ. I'm in the hospital.

He could make out different voices, some female, some male. Pain radiated from his temples to down around his ankles, and he closed his eyes again. Next time he opened them, he saw Cal. Eddie's mouth fell open. In the doorway, dressed in the same plaid shirt and jeans he'd been wearing the night of the accident, stood his kid brother.

"Screwed up, didn't ya? Mom's gonna kill you."

Eddie squinted. "What the hell are you doing here?"

"I'm not here, idiot." The seventeen year old crossed his arms and leaned against the wall. "I'm inside your head. Inside your dreams. Where I've been for the last three years."

A doctor walked by Cal—or *through* Cal, Eddie thought with a shudder—peeling off his gloves as he left the room. No one else even blinked.

"You're dead." Eddie turned his head away. "And I must be close, if I think I'm talking to you."

"Severe lacerations...possible head trauma...hematoma...we need a CAT scan and MRI...X-ray that leg..."

Eddie fought to hold on to the words, to the sentences that swirled around him. But he couldn't even keep his eyes open. Something pricked his arm, and warmth dripped into his veins. He stopped struggling. Even the lights didn't seem so bright anymore.

Better. Doesn't hurt so much. He turned his face back to the doorway. "Still here?"

Cal grinned. "You gotta tell her," he said. His expression grew serious. "You gotta tell her how you feel."

"Who?"

Cal rolled his eyes. "Who do you think? I'm seventeen, not a moron."

"Now you're giving me advice on women?" Eddie found that if he closed his eyes, he could still talk to his brother. Funny. And yet not so funny, after all. Maybe the people closest to you, the ones that wound the threads of their lives through yours, belonged to you forever. Maybe you could continue to have conversations with them. Even past death. Even past hopelessness.

"It's not hopeless," Cal said.

"Stop reading my thoughts."

"Tell her."

"She just got engaged. I saw him put the ring on her finger."

"So?"

"So she's gone. She's not anybody I ever knew, anyway. And she doesn't belong in Paradise."

"That's bullshit."

"Yeah? What do you know?" *Go to hell,* Eddie thought, exhausted.

"Already there, bro. Same place you'll be if you spend your life wondering what would have happened if you'd had the balls to talk to her instead of running away."

"I didn't run away." Eddie didn't want to think about it anymore. He didn't want to hear his dead brother's voice. Didn't want to remember the anguish of saying goodbye at the grave. He felt himself melt into the bed, as if his bones had turned to liquid. As if part of him was already gone. Didn't hurt so much. Besides, if going to sleep, if giving in to the pain and the weakness clamping down on his body meant seeing his brother again for real, then maybe dying wasn't the worst thing in the world.

Maybe everything really did happen for a reason.

* * *

"I'll give you a ride to the hospital," Lacey offered.

Ash shook her head and waited for the room to stop spinning. She wasn't religious, had abandoned church the summer she left for college. But as she hung up the phone, she found herself staring at her fingers, clutching the edge of the bar so hard the tips had all turned white. Would prayer work at a time like this? Did the big guy upstairs listen to people who once vowed never to set foot inside a church again?

"No, it's okay," she said after a minute. "I'll drive myself. I'm okay." And she wondered if God could hear the lies she told out loud too.

Strange, Ash thought as she pulled onto Main Street a few minutes later. She didn't think it had poured this hard all summer. Sure, maybe a quick shower here and there, but nothing so violent. Nothing that made her think that Paradise itself, its streets and its homes along with the people inside them, might be swept off the map. Her fingers shook against the steering wheel. Her stomach churned. She'd had to ask J.T. for directions to the hospital, and even though she'd written them down, she made two wrong turns and had to double back.

"Eddie's been in an accident..."

Again and again she heard the words of his father, the tears bubbling in his voice, the control the man fought to keep. *My God. The Wests had already lost one son.* How could they go through it all again?

She braked hard and swerved to avoid a car abandoned in the middle of the road. Breath hissed through her teeth, and she fought for calm. *Read the directions. Focus on one thing at a time.* Okay, a turn at the blinking yellow light by the highway. A treacherous drive along aptly named River Street. A right turn by the Dairy Dome. Ash started counting breaths, to remind herself to inhale. Another half-mile, and the modest brick building that housed South County Medical Center rose up from the fog. Finally.

She steered into the visitors' lot. Only one other vehicle occupied a spot, a brown pick-up truck with a dent in one side. She ran for the ER doors, which slid open as she approached. In the foyer stood an orderly. He looked her way but didn't speak. She headed for the desk. No one there.

"Hello?" She rapped on the glass divider. After a minute a receptionist appeared, with a sweater pulled tight across her chest. For the first time, Ash realized the room was freezing, with the AC up full blast. She wrapped her arms around herself.

"Eddie West?" The words turned her tongue thick in her mouth. She tried to ask something else but couldn't.

The woman glanced at a chart. "You family?"

Ash shook her head.

"Can't tell you anything. Privacy laws."

She backed away. Had they taken him upstairs, to another room? To surgery? She looked around the waiting area for his father. Not a soul.

"He's asking for you..."

That meant he was okay, right? He wouldn't be talking, or coherent, if he were really that hurt. Without seeing the walls around her, she moved through the waiting room on unsteady legs. In the far corner, she sank onto a blue plastic chair. Two magazines, their covers torn off, lay on a table beside her, and a coffee pot burped in the corner. Otherwise, the place was empty. No emergencies tonight, apparently, except for Eddie. How lucky for everyone else.

Ash closed her eyes. Mistake.

Eddie's mouth on hers, his hands roaming her body, sprang to life behind her lids like it was a motion picture with a viewing audience of one. She stared at the clock above the door instead. Five o'clock. Five-oh-five. Barely the other side of afternoon. On any other day, they'd be sitting on the porch roof talking baseball. They'd be making fun of the neighbors, watching the street, telling stories. They'd be living.

She thought back to their Fourth of July party, counting the days. Two. Four. Five. Five days ago, Eddie and Ash had danced around the porch roof. Later that night, he'd kissed her. And by the next morning, she knew she loved him, somewhere in the back of her mind where the thought was so new it hadn't even opened its eyes.

She tried to glance through a magazine, but the words and pictures blurred. She looked back at the clock and counted the erratic clicks of its old-fashioned hands. The telephone rang. A nurse walked into the waiting room on rubbery white feet, passing Ash without a glance as she pushed her way through the swinging glass door into the area beyond. Into the area, Ash assumed, where they looked patients over, treated their wounds, decided the next and best course of action.

Triage, she thought after a minute. That was the word, the way they decided who was examined first. The one who bled the most got the bandages. But what about injuries that went below the skin? What if you couldn't see how badly you'd broken your heart until it was too late?

"Are you Ashton?" It was a woman's voice, quiet and shaky.

She looked up and saw Eddie's blue eyes. Her heart lurched. "Mrs. West?"

"Irene." The graying brunette sat in the chair beside Ash. She balanced on the edge as if she might jump up again at any moment.

"How is he?"

"They're not sure. He was thrown..." Her last word broke on a sob. A man approached them, and as Ash stood to shake the hand he offered, she saw an older version of Eddie, with the same strong jaw and the same solid stature.

"Malcolm West. Thanks for coming."

She nodded, not sure what she was supposed to say. *I live upstairs from your son? I think I might have fallen in love with him? I've lied to him about everything important since the day we met?*

"They're doing some more tests," Eddie's father said after a minute. He sank into the seat beside his wife and took her hand. "They want to make sure there wasn't any damage to...ah...his brain."

Irene burst into tears and fell against her husband's shoulder.

Ash looked away from them, down at her lap. Black spots circled in front of her eyes, and the room grew hot. Had they turned off the AC? She had to pinch the skin on her arm to keep from passing out.

I shouldn't be here. It's too private, too fragile, too awkward. I don't even know them. I barely know Eddie. She shifted in the chair, meaning to get up, go outside, find some fresh air, when something poked her in the leg. She looked down and saw the bulge in her pocket. The ring. Colin's ring. Colin's offer.

For a minute or two, Ash sat perfectly still. *This is it, the moment I have to choose.* Life with someone she knew, or life with someone she'd only just met. A life that was predictable, that followed rules she knew, or a life with twists and turns she couldn't begin to predict. She ran her fingers across the lump in her pocket and felt the edges of the ring, the smooth circle of the band.

Choosing Colin means I get the marriage I always wanted. I get the comfortable life in Boston. I get the partner my family approves of.

Choosing Eddie means no guarantees. It means taking a chance, holding my breath, and jumping into the deep end. It means starting all over again with someone brand new.

She stole another glance at Eddie's parents. If she said no to Colin, there was no promise Eddie would even know her face when he woke up. Ash stood. "I'm...I'll...would you excuse me?" She reached for her cell phone. "I have to make a phone call."

Irene sniffled and looked at her hands, folded like a broken bird in her lap. Malcolm nodded and tried to smile, but the expression slipped away before it reached his eyes.

Five thirty, the clock now read. Ash found a spot beneath the overhang outside where a weak signal came in. She scrolled down the saved numbers. For a minute she thought about calling Jen, but what good would that do? She couldn't ask her best friend to hop into her car and drive a hundred miles, not on a night like tonight. And not to save Ash from something she needed to figure out by herself.

She stopped halfway down her list and stared at the digits she knew by heart. *It's the right choice. The only choice.* She dialed and waited for Colin to answer.

Chapter Twenty-Seven

"Cal?" Eddie lurched up from unconsciousness. He looked at the door, the last place he'd seen his kid brother. Nothing. No one. Not even a flesh-and-blood doctor or nurse.

His head swam. Everything hurt, tenfold. He rolled his head on the pillow. The bike. The rain. And he'd forgotten the damn helmet. He ran one hand over his thigh and touched gauze. After a minute, he realized his right arm was bounded tightly to his chest. It ached like hell. His hair felt matted against his forehead. *Did I break an arm? Hit face first?* He had no recollection of the accident, no idea how hard he'd hit or how far he'd been thrown.

The room remained empty, and he wondered if they'd moved him up from the ER. He glanced around. Looked like every other damn room in this place, and he'd spent enough time in the hospital to know. The bed next to him was unmade, the hall outside empty. He leaned up on one elbow and caught a glimpse of a sign for the elevator. So he was upstairs. Second floor. That meant his parents were probably wandering the halls somewhere close by. He was surprised Mom wasn't sitting bedside, waiting for him to wake up.

Or maybe she'd figured she couldn't wait like that again. Not after last time.

Tears filled Eddie's eyes, pain he thought he'd gotten rid of long ago. He pressed the first two fingers of his right hand against his breastbone, a gesture from the months after the accident. A superstition. He'd once thought that the hollowness there would go away, that one day when he checked, it would have filled again with something like life. Each day when he woke, for almost a year, he checked for some sign of recovery. Each day his fingers fell away without finding one. After awhile, he realized they never would. Like a bum ankle, or a scar that stretched the length of your jaw line, some pain you carried around with you forever.

But tonight it wasn't there. Surprised, he closed his eyes and checked again. That awful emptiness, that bone-deep ache that had greeted him each morning for the last three years, had disappeared. Maybe the accident had shaken it loose. Maybe grief had run its course. Or maybe he'd finally met someone who cast light on him again.

He reached for the call button. Cal was right. He had to let Ash know how he felt. *She's the reason I didn't roll over and die.* She had to be. Nothing else had changed in Paradise this summer, except for her coming here.

Eddie only hoped it wasn't too late to tell her that.

* * *

"Thanks for meeting me here."

Colin ducked under the overhang. Rain dripped onto the back of his neck and soaked his shirt. "No problem."

Ash crossed her arms over her chest and shivered.

"How's your friend?"

She shook her head, not trusting herself to guess.

"Ash." He took hold of her arms and pulled her close.

She blinked away tears. Fitting herself against Colin's chest, the way she had so many times before, felt right. It felt familiar. She knew his rough spots and his edges. She knew the way he slept with one leg outside the covers and the way he ordered his eggs in the morning. She knew the feeling of his arm around her when they stood for pictures. And as if the pages of her life had suddenly opened in front of her, Ash saw the next forty years with Colin. She saw a lavish wedding, a house in the suburbs, children, a dog, and vacations to Europe.

She saw TV interviews and reporters. Elections and sound bites. She saw Congressional balls and fund-raising banquets. She saw her own law practice grow and then fade as she gave it up to support her husband's presidential hopes. She saw all the things she wasn't sure she wanted.

"You made a decision." He whispered the words into her hair, a statement rather than a question.

Ash nodded into the soft fabric of his shirt. Even without looking at her, he knew.

"You're in love with him." Another statement.

"I'm sorry."

"Don't be." Colin pulled away from her and squeezed her hand. "It's not your fault. It's mine. I screwed up. Waited too long." He glanced over his shoulder, at the parking lot, the sky, the tops of the buildings that marked downtown Paradise. When he looked back at her again, a careful mask had dropped into place.

She reached into her pocket. "Here."

Colin nodded as he slipped the ring into the folds of his palm.

"It's beautiful," she said. "But for someone else. You belong with someone else." Her chest lifted and felt lighter even as she said the words.

"I guess I'll see you around," Colin said. He scratched his jaw. "Back in the city, maybe. If you go home."

"I'll be there," Ash said and meant it. She watched as he got into his car and pulled away without looking back.

Yes, she needed to go back to Boston. But not now. Not right away. There was something she had to do here in Paradise first.

* * *

"Don't cry, Ma." Eddie patted her hand. "I'm gonna be fine. Doc said."

Irene West drew a deep breath. Tears traced a familiar path down both cheeks. Behind her, Eddie's father stood with his back to the room, looking out onto an evening that had finally cleared.

"Goddamn fool." The man spoke to the window, but Eddie heard his anger, loud and clear. "Didn't learn a damn thing from your brother's death, huh? Thought maybe you'd be better off in the ground beside him?"

"Dad, I—" What was he supposed to say? He hadn't gone out looking for the accident to happen. He hadn't planned it, for Christ's sake. Eddie looked at his mother, who continued to weep, and wondered if the tears were for him or for Cal.

Ash had never known him. Eddie was startled to feel relief rather than regret. She'd never cried for him. Never compared Eddie to Cal. And she was the one person in Paradise who didn't see the kid brother he'd killed every time she looked at him.

It was, he realized suddenly, one more reason he'd fallen for her.

"I'm not him. I'm not Cal." He paused. "And I'm not dead."

His father turned. For a long moment, he stared at his son. "Your friend's here."

Eddie frowned. "Frank?"

"The woman. The one you kept asking for. Ashton."

The name struck Eddie square in the heart. "I asked for her?" Impossible. He would have remembered. He would have felt her name on his tongue.

His mother managed a weak smile. "A couple of times. The nurse on duty knew who she was. Told us to call the restaurant."

"And she came?" *Even after I acted like a jerk, ran away like I was twelve years old?*

His father nodded. "She's been here a while."

Irene turned. "But she's..." She pressed her lips together and shook her head at her husband.

"What?" Eddie caught the look that passed between them.

Suddenly he knew. The machine monitoring his blood pressure beeped a couple of times. *Colin. She's here with Colin. Of course.* Again he saw the guy down on one knee. Eddie coughed. Well, it made sense that he'd come to the hospital with Ash. He probably gave her a ride, held her hand in consolation while she did her duty and checked on her neighbor.

"Do you want me to see if she's still downstairs?" Eddie's father moved toward the door. "I'm sure she'd like to see you."

Eddie yanked up the thin blanket that had bunched around his knees. All he really wanted to do now was sleep. He felt like an idiot, calling out some woman's name while he was delirious with pain. Especially when the woman in question had shown up at the hospital with another guy.

"Nah. Don't bother. You can tell her thanks, but she can go on home." It was better that way. Better for both of them, if they never saw each other again.

Chapter Twenty-Eight

"He's upstairs. Room 214."

Ash stood in the waiting room, where Malcolm West had found her pacing and biting her bottom lip. "He's okay?"

"He will be." The man smiled for the first time since she'd arrived at the hospital. "He's pretty banged up. Suffered a concussion, a broken ankle, and a dislocated collarbone. Lost a lotta skin, too, but the doc says he'll be fine. He's very lucky."

Ash wiped her hands on her shorts. Looking down, she realized she still wore her work clothes and still had her hair up in an unwashed ponytail.

"...said he didn't want to see you," Eddie's father finished saying.

"He...what?" Eddie didn't want to see her? But he'd asked for her. He'd wanted her to come to the hospital. Hadn't he?

"But I think that's the drugs talking." Malcolm led Ash toward the elevators. "I know my son." His voice turned gruff. "Maybe not as well as I oughta. But I know you mean something to him." The elevator doors slid open, and they stepped inside. "I knew from the look on his face when his mother told him you were down here with someone else."

"You..." *You weren't supposed to see that*, she finished silently.

He cocked his head and looked at her for a moment. "You're the senator's daughter, aren't you?"

She nodded. No reason to hide anymore.

"He's a good man, got caught in a bad spot," Malcolm said. "You can tell 'im I said that. Hope he doesn't let it keep him down."

Ash smiled at the kindness in the man's words. "I don't think he will. We Kirks are pretty tough when we need to be." The elevator doors creaked open, and she could see room 214 to her right.

The older man's hand rested on her shoulder for a moment as they stepped into the hall. "He looks a little rough right now. Just so you know."

"He's awake?"

Eddie's mother slipped out of the room and came toward them. "He's drowsy," she said in response to Ash's question. "But yes. He's awake."

Ash left them standing in the hallway and forced herself to walk toward Eddie's room. With one hand, she knocked, pushed open the door, and stepped inside.

Oh, Eddie.

For a moment she couldn't speak. She could barely draw a full breath. Someone had cut off the T-shirt he'd been wearing, and he sat up against the pillows with a bare chest and scrapes along his chin. One foot looked lumpy under the sheets. The edges of a purple bruise puffed out around one eye, and his right arm lay strapped in a sling across his chest.

But it was him. It was Eddie, whole and alive and looking at her with something in his gaze she couldn't quite read. Anger? Relief? Happiness? Affection?

Neither one spoke. *He's still angry.* And he had every right to be. Between her father waking them up and her ex-boyfriend reappearing with a marriage proposal, she imagined that, quite possibly, Eddie wouldn't want anything to do with her again.

"Why the hell did you take off like that? In the middle of a storm?" They weren't the words she'd meant to say, rough with anger and fear. But they were the first ones that came out.

He frowned. "Got about a hundred questions I could ask you, too."

Ash hunched her shoulders. She'd screwed up. In her mind's eye, she saw dark red hair, an hourglass figure, a local girl who'd soothed Eddie after the loss of his brother. Maybe he wanted someone like Cass, someone who didn't lie about her background. Maybe he wanted someone who'd grown up with him, who knew all the secrets of the town. Maybe he wanted someone to climb on the back of a bike at a moment's notice and toss her hair across his lap.

Ash didn't have hair that tossed.

"My mom said you were here with someone."

She nodded. "I was." *Truth. Only the truth from here on in.*

"So where is he?"

She shrugged. "He left. Went back to Boston."

"Yeah?" Eddie ran a hand through his hair.

"Yeah."

I love you. The notion prickled her skin, startled her, terrified her, and yet the longer she stood there, the longer she knew it to be true. All the nights they'd spent on the porch, all the drinks they'd shared at the bar, all the afternoons eating grilled cheese and watching the Red Sox: they'd become all the little puzzle pieces that made up a love, and a life.

Eddie was her best friend, the one who caught her when she fell, who made her laugh until the corners of her mouth ached, who danced her to sleep under a midnight moon. He was the one who knew Ash the woman, not Ash the Kirk daughter, and not Ash the Harvard grad. He was the one who lived with her and put up with her. The one who loved her for the complicated person she was. The one who made her happy.

"If I could take it back…if I could change the things I said, the things I told you at the beginning, I would…" She trailed off. "I would have started the summer over," she went on after a moment.

"I would have told you the truth from the start." *I wouldn't have tried to build a whole life on a lie.*

Eddie didn't say anything. Ash walked to the bed, and her legs brushed the sheet that fell over the side. From up close she could see the fatigue around his eyes, the glassiness in his expression, the scratches and scrapes along his arms. She stood beside him and held her breath. One second. Two. His free hand crawled across the blanket to hers.

"You asked them to call me?"

"Apparently." He grinned. "Though I was pretty drugged up, so I might have asked for the Queen of England too."

"Not Cass?"

"Come on. What do you think?" Eddie shook his head. "It's always been you, Ash. From the day we moved in, I think." He chuckled. "You didn't even give me a chance, just reeled me in and made me fall."

"But I lied about so much." She wanted everything out in the open, every last bit of the ragged edges that needed mending.

"You had your reasons, I guess." He lifted her hand to his lips.

"I'm so sorry. You need to know how sorry I am."

"I already do." He glanced at her other hand, the one without the diamond on it. "You're here, right?"

She nodded. "Yeah. And I'm not going anywhere."

He relaxed his hold, and his eyes fluttered. "Good." His breathing deepened, and he tugged her close. "Ashton Kirk."

"What?"

"Stay with me."

She laced her fingers through his. "I will."

"Tonight?"

She laughed. "I'm not sure they'll let me. I'd have to sweet-talk one of the nurses."

But he was shaking his head. "Tomorrow. And the next day. And after the leaves fall. And next spring. Stay in Paradise with me."

Ash didn't answer. She wasn't sure she could. But one thing she knew for certain: whether she stayed here in New Hampshire, or convinced Eddie to move to Boston, whether she moved to Europe to follow a job or opened a restaurant with him in another corner of the country, she wasn't ever leaving.

I found myself here just when I thought I'd lost everything

She'd didn't need to run anymore, didn't need to hide. She didn't need to pretend away her name. She didn't need to be anything except a woman who was completely in love with the boy next door. Ash smiled and bent to kiss Eddie's forehead as he drifted into sleep.

"Yes," she whispered. "I'll stay."

Paradise, she'd tuck into her heart no matter where they ended up. She'd have it with her. Always.

One Year Later...

"Where's this party, anyway?" Ash asked as Jen turned down unfamiliar streets. She'd only been to Newburg Heights a couple of times. Located halfway between Boston and Paradise, it was bigger than Paradise, a little farther from the junior college and a little more wealthy, if Ash could judge by the homes they'd passed since leaving the highway.

"Lucas gave me directions. Here." Jen passed her a crumpled slip of paper.

"Whatever happened to GPS?"

"Stop grumbling," Jen laughed as they turned down a narrow street lined with bungalows.

"What was Lucas doing up here, anyway?" Seemed like kind of a far commute from central Connecticut.

"Helping a friend do some renovations." Jen jabbed a finger at the paper. "Now read, would ya?"

"Fine." Ash recited directions until they dead-ended in front of a small, white ranch-style house at the end of a cul-de-sac. The house had a wider, greener lawn than some of the others on the block, and low flowering bushes lined the walk leading up to the front door.

Ash frowned. "What's Eddie doing here? He told me he was working late."

Jen shrugged and pulled up to the curb. "You ready?"

Her stomach rumbled. "I guess." Teaching a morning Constitutional Law class at the junior college, followed by a busy lunch crowd at the restaurant, had left her starving. A barbeque to celebrate whatever construction project Lucas had just finished sounded like the perfect way to end a long week. "How's your brother doing, anyway?" she asked as she climbed from the car. "Got a girlfriend yet?"

Jen checked her makeup in the rear view mirror. "Nah. Goes on a date here and there, but you know him. Mr. Strong and Silent isn't exactly gonna jump into another serious relationship. He's waitin' for the right one to come along, that's all." She glanced at Ash. "Not everyone gets as lucky as you and Eddie."

"I know." She twisted her fingers in her lap. *Still takes my breath away, every time I see him.* She glanced at the front porch, where he leaned against a porch column beside Lucas, talking and laughing. Broad shoulders and slim hips that knew her hands and fit against her own bare skin just right...

"Come on." Jen climbed from the car, and Ash followed, heat spiraling from her cheeks to her toes. Didn't look like there were a lot of people here for the party, but maybe most of the guests were arriving later. Maybe she could sneak Eddie away for a few minutes, find a dark corner and wind herself around him until her fatigue went away and she tingled from his touch. Jen stopped her before they got to the walk. "Hang on." She swept Ash's hair from her forehead and inspected her for a long moment.

"What the hell are you doing?"

"Okay, you'll pass."

"Pass what?"

"Good call on that dress. It actually makes you look like you have some curves."

Ash glanced down at the red mini-dress she'd bought in the spring. A little skimpy for her taste, but – "Eddie likes this one."

"I'll bet he does." Jen steered her up the walk. "Now go."

"Wait, what are you – " But when Ash turned around, Jen's torso was bent over the trunk among a half-dozen bags and boxes.

"Be right there," she called.

Ash shrugged. Whatever. "Hi handsome," she said to Eddie as she neared the porch. Lucas had disappeared somewhere, probably around back if she had to guess, from the aroma of grilled meat wafting out to them. Fresh red paint on the front door and impatiens lining the windows gave the house an inviting air. A Cape-style with dormers, it sat low to the ground, cozy and warm, like something she'd choose for herself one day. "Cute place. Did you help too?" She didn't recalled Eddie mentioning it, but they'd both been so busy this last month that it might have slipped by her.

"I helped a little, yeah." He ran a hand over the porch railing. "You like it?

"It's nice. Very cute. Did Frank close the shop early today?"

Eddie rubbed the back of his neck. "Ah, yeah." Hair damp from the shower, shirt a little wrinkled, he smelled as delicious as always, and for a second Ash thought about suggesting they find a bedroom to christen rather than pull up picnic chairs. Damn, he turned her hot in a hurry. She reached for him, but rather than fold her into his arms, he stepped back.

"What's wrong?"

His face reddened. "Nothin'. Just – ah. Close your eyes for a minute, will ya?"

"Close my – " She stopped. Jen's knowing look. Eddie being here in the middle of the afternoon. Her pulse sped up as she closed her eyes, lids trembling against the sunlight.

"Okay."

When she opened her eyes again, Eddie rested before her, one knee to the ground and a box in his hand. Ash started to cry.

"Told you a long time ago that you changed my life." His voice broke on the opening words. He opened the box, and a gorgeous diamond surrounded by two sapphires sparkled in the afternoon light. "It's always been you, Ash. Always."

She cried harder. Somewhere behind her she thought she heard voices, but she didn't trust her legs to turn around.

"You are my best friend. My soul mate. You are my world, my light, everything good that's ever happened to me. Please say you'll marry me."

She couldn't speak. *I came to Paradise to escape. Who knew I'd end up finding everything I'd ever wanted?* She nodded, not trusting her voice.

"Is that a yes?"

"Yes," she managed to say as he slid the ring onto her finger. "Oh, Eddie, yes. Forever, a thousand times, yes."

"It's about time," Jen said from behind her. She skipped over and grabbed Ash's hand. "Damn. Must have cost a fortune, Lover Boy." She planted a kiss on Eddie's cheek. "Congrats."

Ash stared at her hand in wonder, but for a moment only, as other familiar faces joined them in the front yard. "Dad?" And her mother too, and both her sisters. "You – " She turned back to Eddie. "You invited them all here?" There was Frank and his wife, and a couple of waitresses from the restaurant, and Shelia and Teagan, her fellow professors from the college. "All of them?"

"Yeah. Good thing you said yes. Woulda been a shitty party if you hadn't." This time, finally, he pulled her in for a kiss, one hand in her hair and the other tight around her waist.

On her tiptoes she leaned into him. Their kiss deepened, and her hands moved to his face, to the stubble of his beard she loved so much. "I'm crazy about you," she whispered against him.

He ran one hand over her hair, his expression tender as his thumb rested on her lower lip. "Any chance I can convince you to sneak away for a quickie before the party starts?"

She laughed. *You read my mind.* "I don't know if the host would be thrilled with that." She glanced at the front door. "Though I wouldn't mind taking a tour of the house. What do you say we ask?"

Eddie let her go long enough to pull a key from his pocket. "He says yes."

Ash looked at the key, attached to a fob that read "Frank's Imports." She'd seen that fob before – or one like it, anyway. Her brows drew together. "I don't..." Realization spread over her. She looked from Eddie to Lucas and back again. "Please tell me you are not the 'friend' that Lucas came up here to help."

Lucas grinned from under his baseball cap and held up both palms. "Guilty."

"Eddie!" Her jaw dropped. "This is *your* house?"

"Actually, it's our house, now that you said yes." He twisted the key in the door. "And I'm pretty sure the party can wait until we take ourselves a tour of it."

* * *

Much later, after the last guests had driven away and the grill was cold and she'd hugged Jen goodbye and promised to call as soon as the dress search began, Ash followed Eddie into the back bedroom, the master, the only one with furniture and the only one that needed it tonight, as far as she was concerned.

"To the future," he whispered. "And to my beautiful wife."

Not yet, she almost corrected him, but it didn't matter because in soul she already was. Linked to him, loving him, she'd known too from that first day that he was her One, the single person she'd been seeking. Every day, every minute of the rest of her life, wouldn't be long enough to spend with him.

By degrees he pulled the neckline of her dress away from her skin, replacing each inch with his mouth. Teasing. Wet. She arched into his touch, bottom lip caught in her teeth. One hand caught her nipple, running the thumb over and over until it hardened and she cried out in want. With gentle hands he lowered her to the bed, and in the next moment Eddie slipped off her dress entirely and tossed it aside. He pulled his own shirt over his head and dropped it onto the floor. His shorts followed. Then, in slow degrees, his hands returned to her skin. He grinned, his dimple popping under those sky-blue eyes, but he didn't say anything. His fingers moved to her belly, to her legs, to the smooth, warm, desperately wet apex that ached for his touch.

"Eddie..." She reached for him, legs and arms and tongues entwined, and then it was like always, coming without even feeling him inside her yet, rolling on that wave until another one came after it and finally she pulled him into her because if she didn't she would die, it was as simple as that.

Completion. Utter completion, she thought a while later as they lay together in silence. "I love you."

"Oh, Ash. Times a thousand. Times a million." He rolled up and rested on one elbow. "I'm the luckiest guy in the world. To get to spend every day with you, to come home every night to you..." Tears stood in his eyes. "You saved me."

Wasn't it amazing, she thought as she wound her fingers through his, how two people could save each other? Could love each other, complete each other, catch each other when they fell and steady each other against the storms of the world around them?

Eddie lifted her fingers to his lips. Her ring glittered in the half-light. "I'll go to the moon and back to make you happy. Fill up every ocean. I promise, I'll tell the world a hundred times a day how lucky I am that I get to be loved by you."

Ash closed her eyes, emotion turning into a tight little ball at the back of her throat. No words. Just love. How amazing.

"Me too," she agreed. "Every day. I promise."

Want to find out if Lucas discovers his true love?
Read *Beacon of Love* coming in May 2013!

* * *

Beacon of Love
Excerpt

"Wise ass." Sophie backed into the street before Lucas could grab her. "I'll see you later!" she called. "I think Lon said something about meeting tomorrow morning and--hey!" She squawked off the last word as Lucas lifted her off the ground and onto his shoulder.

As if she was a bag of flour.

Or a damsel in distress.

Or his damn cavewoman.

About a hundred thoughts raced through her mind, and it took all she had to keep them from coming out in biting words.

"Why do you have to be so stubborn?" Lucas asked as he carried Sophie back to his truck, parked in front of the bar. He wasn't panting, not out of breath in the least, as if she weighed close to nothing. "If anything happened to you, Lon would kill me." With one hand he opened the passenger side door. Only then did he lower her to a seat inside the truck. His hands slid down her arms and settled her hips into place.

Oh yum. All her scathing thoughts of thirty seconds earlier vanished. She shifted on the leather. There was room for him on this side of the cab, she was almost positive. If not, she'd make room. In about two seconds...

Available from www.lyricalpress.com in May 2013

About the Author

Allie Boniface is a small-town girl at heart who's traveled around the world and still finds that the magic and the mystery of small towns make them the best places to fall in love and find adventure. From the New England coast to Rocky Mountain hotels to tiny European bars, she's found more character and plot inspirations than she could ever count. Currently, she's lucky enough to live in New York's beautiful Hudson Valley with her own romance hero, her husband who can fix, build, drive, and grill anything and is the epitome of the strong and silent type.

When she isn't writing love stories, Allie is a full-time high school English teacher who enjoys helping her teenagers negotiate the ups and downs of writing along with the ups and downs of life (because, really, she's still trying to do the same thing!). And while she'll continue to travel far and wide, Allie knows there's really nothing like coming back to the place where the people who have known you welcome you home with open arms.

You can keep up with all of Allie's news and new releases on Facebook, Twitter, or at www.allieboniface.com.

Printed in Great Britain
by Amazon